FUNERAL MUSIC
FOR FREEMASONS

Also by Lars Gustafsson

The Death of a Beekeeper
(Translated by Janet K. Swaffar
and Gustram H. Weber)

The Tennis Players
(Translated by Yvonne L. Sandstroem)

Sigismund
(Translated by John Weinstock)

Stories of Happy People
(Translated by Yvonne L. Sandstroem
and John Weinstock)

LARS GUSTAFSSON

FUNERAL MUSIC
FOR FREEMASONS

TRANSLATED FROM THE SWEDISH
BY YVONNE L. SANDSTROEM

A NEW DIRECTIONS BOOK

Originally published as *Sorgemusik för frimurare* P. A. Nordstedt & Söners Förlag, Stockholm, in 1983. This English translation is published by arrangement with Carl Hanser Verlag, Munich.

Manufactured in the United States of America
First published clothbound and as New Directions Paperback 636 in 1987
Published simultaneously in Canada by Penguin Books Canada Limited

Library of Congress Cataloging-in-Publication Data
Gustafsson, Lars, 1936–
    Funeral Music for Freemasons.
    (A New Directions Book)
    Translations of: Sorgemusik för frimurare.
    I. Sandstroem, Yvonne L. II. Title.
PT9876.17.U8S6513 1987   839.7'374   86-28655
ISBN 0-8112-1017-0
ISBN 0-8112-1018-9 (pbk.)

New Directions Books are published for James Laughlin
by New Directions Publishing Corporation,
80 Eighth Avenue, New York 10011

They know freedom, if freedom
is a wind that carries far away.
At night they separate from one another.
Their shared day is brief.
At night you see them ride
the clouds above us.
None by the other's side.
No traces. No torches.

Lars Forssell, from "Lettre Sentimentale," *Telegram*, 1957

CONTENTS

1   The River

1

The river, with a smell suddenly gray, infinitely broad, is right now disappearing into the encircling fog just before sunup.

Days like that the river—impossible to survey, gray and sluggish under its gray, tropical Laplandish sky—desires hardly anything. Under a cloud of restlessly circling purple herons fresh fog rises continually from the water. While a flock of storks clacks restlessly in the sick, shadowy water of the baolongs, the saltwater channels, behind high grass I cannot see, the river glides on, carrying everyone with equal composure.

For two years I had sailed with tourists between the Hotel Diola in Ziguinchor and the mouth of the river, two-day tours for the most part. Occasionally, when required, I'd sail further away. The *Amedée* was a comfortable boat. It had belonged to the last French governor in Casamance Basse and had three cabins. The boy, whom I always called Monsieur Bée and whose real name was something different, always slept in the forepeak. It was the birds that interested the Frenchmen the most. The Americans wanted to go to villages like Karabane and Diembereng: small, low houses with grass roofs, mortars for pounding millet that reached to the women's armpits, black pigs, and friendly voices. The Diolas are a beautiful and friendly people. I know many of them. They know me.

This time I was only bringing two tourists back. We had had four on the way out. There was nothing strange about it. Not uncommonly, people prefer to disembark for a few days in Cape Skiring. They can then fly straight back to Dakar or else return by rented car to Ziguinchor on the new motor way, over Santiaba Mandjak and Oussoye. This appeals to many people. The first stretch of the road, approximately at the level of Essoukoudiak, runs perfectly parallel to the border of Guinea-Bissau.

Monsieur Bée had woken us with coffee at six o'clock, at Pointe Saint Georges. On board were a *nouveau riche* gentleman and his blond wife or girlfriend. Rather pleasant people from Nevers. It had proved quite impossible to sail during the night, something I usually prefer to do since I am easily disturbed and a poor sleeper. The engine penetrates my sleep. Its sound colors my dreams.

In addition, there is something I refer to as my "sleep injury." I don't know when it appeared. It has been with me for a long time. It is an empty cavity in my sleep, a white nothingness, occurring between four and five in the morning. If I try to fill it with something—reading, for instance—it grows into an enormous thing and continues until morning.

This empty time contains absolutely nothing. I have no name, no identity, for as long as it persists. Still, I sometimes believe that it's a trick I have invented in order to keep myself anchored to myself.

When the fog lifts the wind always comes. We could easily have set sail, but we were almost there. Soon after Iles aux Oiseaux, the long bridge appears, the fog lifts, the sun is like a burning glass against your forehead.

The Estrée family, if they were a family, were already sitting in canvas chairs on deck, greedy for sun. This afternoon they would be in light, open Dakar with its friendly sea breezes, and after that they'd be in Europe, where it was still early March.

The low white harbor buildings, the giant baobab tree outside the Labor Exchange, and the alley where the slaves had once taken their last walk down to the slave ships would show up any moment in the morning light. I pointed out the right bank to them, the starboard side, where the Dutch tried to plant rice a few years back but ended up with a salt marsh. I myself have seen the enormous quantities of soil that were needed to reinforce the road that would carry their machines. That it wouldn't succeed is something anyone could have told them.

We docked around eight.

While Monsieur Bée moored the boat and put out the fenders, I accepted the guests' checks and helped them ashore.

There were the usual people on the pier, some men fishing with rods and the usual small boys; in addition there were two police officers. They were not the police officers commonly seen in Ziguinchor. Up the narrow street two cars were parked in such a way that it was impossible to get through, one an ordinary police car and the other some kind of jeep.

If a political coup had occurred there'd be some sense to it, but as everyone knows, there are no political coups in Senegal.

4

The officers looked over the railing politely, two rather shy Diola youths perspiring heavily under their kepis; I nodded to them in a friendly manner and went on with my job of straightening up on board.

They really have to be green, I thought, since they haven't even seen a sailboat before. I smiled at them invitingly. The younger one returned my smile cautiously.

It takes quite a while to put a ketch in order. There is leftover food that has to be thrown away, and there are a number of locks to lock. Even though Monsieur Bée always sleeps on board, he would spend all afternoon with friends in Ziguinchor. You can easily be robbed.

I have to admit that I forgot about those two officers for a while; I was slightly irritated to see them still standing there when I jumped ashore with my small garbage bag and my other, much smaller, canvas bag.

One of them took my bags with surprising speed, and the other one put the handcuffs on me.

Only then did I realize that I had made my last trip. On the way to the car—already a group of small boys and an assortment of idle, roaming younger men, regarding us matter-of-factly, had started gathering—I thought, Good Lord, how hot the car will be after standing there all morning.

One of them held the door for me—Diolas are always polite—the other threw the bags beside me on the back seat.

"But it's garbage," I said. "Nothing but garbage—"

Nobody laughed. Nobody seemed interested in checking that I was actually telling the truth.

The police station in Ziguinchor bears a resemblance to an aquarium. It's because of the green walls, absolutely sea green, with stucco that's peeling in places but which still retains its green color in some way or other. The large fans rotating on the ceiling are reminiscent of the shadows in an aquarium. There was the usual long row of visitors, all black: someone who'd had a chicken stolen on a bus and was complaining loudly; someone who had lost his bicycle; a boy who had stolen a tourist's wallet. Everyone quarreled with everyone else.

They brought me straight to the prefect, Monsieur Basseré.

I know him well. He has an incredibly fat wife who comes from Kubanao, and he is a strict Sufi.

"My dear Basseré," I said.

This time he was not smiling.

"My dear Basseré, please explain to your boys that one of the bags, the paper one, is full of garbage and that it will smell to high heaven if they don't throw it out. And then I'd be grateful if they'd remove these handcuffs. You can't possibly imagine that I'd start a fight with you."

He left the bags standing by his desk. The handcuffs were removed.

"Thank you, Monsieur Basseré," I said. "Do you have any idea why you have had me arrested? If it's my residency permit you don't have to use handcuffs, do you now? If there are problems I am always ready to discuss them. Is there some kind of problem with my boat?"

He looked up at the ceiling where the same kind of fan as the one in the waiting room threw the same kind of shadow. A dull room, with an old table stained brown, metal cabinets and wooden roll-front cabinets, an ancient picture, probably a school photo, and his uniform jacket hanging over a chair.

"I have to hold you," he said joylessly.

"Then I'd like to know what I'm suspected of," I said.

"You sailed four days ago."

"To Cape Skiring."

"You had two passengers on board who did not return with you?"

"You mean those nice young Germans?"

"They looked in very good shape. Like baseball players."

"Yes, they did seem to be in good shape. You saw them, then?"

"I did. Where are they now?"

"That I don't know. Sunbathing in Cape Skiring I suppose. Or else they've rented a car. I didn't throw them overboard, I can assure you of that."

"I didn't think you had."

"Then why am I here?"

"You know quite well what I believe."

"Listen," I said. "Call the governor."

6

"I know that you're a close friend of Governor Diakene Oulof," Prefect Basseré said. "But you will not be able to reach him."

"It's my legal right to write to him if I consider that your jail is being mismanaged, for instance."

"My jail is very well run. We've just had the ceilings fumigated."

"Why?"

"Cockroaches. What did you think?"

He allowed himself a laugh, a large, open laugh that was Wolof rather than Diola. "You're welcome to see the governor. If you can. But he isn't here. He's been called to Dakar."

"When will he be back?"

"You know what it's like with government cars . . ."

"Nonsense, he'll fly."

"How do you know that he's coming back?"

For the first time I felt real uneasiness. Things must be more serious than I had supposed. I must have been silent long enough for Basseré to notice. How much did he know? He would never tell me now.

"Let me take down your particulars," he said.

He made quite a production of picking up one of the thin forms, smoothing the corners that had curled from the humid heat, discarding it, and then picking up another one before finally, soberly, inserting it into the typewriter.

"You know that my name is Jan Bohman," I said. "And that I own a travel agency and a grocery store."

"Place and date of birth, please."

"Stockholm, 1936, May 17th."

"That's in Oslo?"

"No, Monsieur Basseré, Stockholm is in Sweden. Really now, when do you suppose the governor will return?"

"I think that depends on whether he will return at all."

The cell was probably the best one he had, with unbroken bedsprings and a strong odor of insecticide and old, oxidized urine. The window was placed high in the wall, but mercifully it had no glass, just a grille.

I lay there thinking while the light from the window traveled across the room.

Things looked bad.

Strictly speaking, however, it might have been worse. A great deal worse, as a matter of fact. The most interesting thing right now was neither the cell nor the insistent smell of urine, not even the moving shaft of light and the sound of the police station cook, evidently busying himself cooking millet porridge for the prisoners in a pot that had to be somewhere close by—commonplace sounds and smells, mild signals which told me that I was still in the world of the living.

The most interesting fact was that I was still in a condition to observe them.

Someone, far away in the ramifications of a menacing and labyrinthine reality, a reality that did not have much in common with the ordinary world but which still, in a way, *was* the ordinary world, that someone must have had some momentary good intentions toward me.

2

I don't know what made me think of the poem. I can't have thought of it for a very long time.

I woke up from my shallow morning sleep, still in my cell. Someone knocked discreetly on the door, took away my chamber pot, put down a tin mug of coffee, and left me alone once more. It must have been about half past six: the light stood rose-colored in the window opening.

Today I might find out, but probably wouldn't, if the governor had returned. If it was the same governor, that is to say. If it wasn't the same governor but a different one, then I was in bad trouble.

I'd heard the poem for the first time the spring of 1958, in a smoke-filled garret in Uppsala, in the old wooden house down by the river called Imperfect Tense. (I wonder if it's still there.) It may have been a meeting of *Upbeat*'s editorial board; in that case it was at Göran and Tora's. May, but doesn't have to have been. I remember the room as very smoky and that there were two girls who interested me equally. One was dark and a bit plump, a little sad, you might say, sad or maybe simply more on the quiet side. The other one was blond, somewhat more talkative, very sensitive, very restless. Both of them wrote poetry. And then there was a guy who talked continuously about Wagner versus Brahms, as if they were two worlds at war with one another. (Perhaps he was right. Perhaps there are musical worlds that are actually at war with one another.)

What I remember is that it must have been the first day above freezing that year, 1958.

Some of us had run into each other around three in the afternoon, just by chance. It was down by Gustavianum, and the melted snow was running at the curb. Picklas and Gustav had just come from one of Teddy Brunius' lectures. When I ran into them they had just started talking to a girl with long, beautiful hair and cheekbones that were a bit too hard. Her name was Kerstin. I didn't know her. She wore funny earrings made from brass or copper, and I remember Picklas asking her "whether they'd been approved by Teddy Brunius." There was a lot of stuff about esthetics, about taste, in the air at that time. Perhaps it was a form of fear.

Just for fun, we started sailing wooden matches in the gutter, matches that we marked in different ways and which might have all kinds of adventures on their way down to the sewer, which was the end of their career, so to speak. It might be a sand bar, a bit of gray snow protruding like a roof over the current. There were two tickets for the Fyris Cinema, the seven o'clock show, an empty book of food coupons for Delmonico's student dining hall, torn straight across, and an empty pack of Boy cigarettes; in one spot, there was an empty, unrinsed milk bottle that forced the whole current down into the street. It wasn't that easy, either, to keep track of your particular match.

The whole thing might seem childish, but this was at a time when it was permissible to be childish. Manne came down the street with his rolling gait, in a poplin raincoat and a large blue scarf, his head gloriously empty after an important exam in logic. That spring, he was working on his doctorate in theoretical philosophy. Just as the rest of us were beginning to lose interest, he started in earnest.

All of them thought it was kind of fun that I'd joined them. I was a few years older, but above all it was because my first book of poems, *River Nights*, had been published by Metamorfos Press the previous fall. It had had, as the saying went in those days, a glowing reception. I had given a reading at Värmland's Student Association, also on the radio, and I was on the editorial boards of both *Upbeat* and *Salamander*. I was simply the new Uppsala poet, perhaps the new Swedish poet, and I enjoyed it. I would have a whole admiring crowd around my table at Café Alma. In addition, I was Victor Svanberg's graduate assistant in the Department of Literary History.

I remember quite well how the rest of the day went. Manne went on his way, but Picklas, I, and a few other people decided to have dinner at the City Hotel. In those days, fifty kronor would do it. Of course it had to be the City Hotel, because the Gillet's Bar was full of people who'd sit there all evening, shouting to make themselves heard.

We got there so early it was almost empty. All on his own, the piano player had started on an arrangement of "Moonlight Serenade"; sunlight was still coming in through large windows, sharp March light that hurt your eyes, and Picklas was just telling a funny story about what Knaggen had said to Victor about Sven's dissertation when they came in.

That must have been the way it happened. And that must have been how the poem turned up the first time.

They sauntered in, barely speaking to each other. And that was the first time I saw Hasse and Ann-Marie Nöhme, Hasse big and heavy, the way I always see him in my mind's eye, dressed in a blazer (but not without elegance) and Ann-Marie, so short, with short, very short, ash-blond hair, a rounded figure in a gray cotton dress that looked almost like a nurse's uniform. Boyish and feminine at the same time.

I can assure you, from that moment I saw nothing else in the room. She felt it, and we looked at one another. Hasse must have felt it, too. He marched over to our table right away, in a manner that was typical of him (something I didn't know at the time) and asked if there was anything in particular I wanted.

10

It was a test, and everybody knew it. He didn't actually look that strong, but I didn't like the expression in his eyes; I've never cared for fights in public places. Also, there was something sad in his eyes. Good Lord! I never thought of that! But perhaps he realized that he was beaten, even then.

"You're right," I said. "There is something I want. I'd like to suggest that you join us so we can buy you a glass of wine."

Immediately he became doubtful. He'd already lost the initiative, lost the rhythm, and was helplessly suspended between roles.

"Why?" he asked.

"Because you look so lonesome," I said.

What was there to do? Already I'd practically won. They came over. He'd driven up from Stockholm, in his own car. He was a research physicist at the Royal Technical College, and she? She was a student at the Opera, she told me.

That was the first time I heard her voice. It was like a silver bell: very clear, but with a touch of coldness. I believe that small impersonal tinge was something which would later become a hindrance in her career. It was a voice of precision and strength, but the critics would keep returning to this: it lacked "warmth."

Of course it isn't easy to say what constitutes "warmth." There was a kind of sadness in her voice, no, not sadness, something different, perhaps a primordial conviction that nothing in the world is of any real significance, but something was lost, once and for all, at the moment of birth.

Her eyes bore a strange resemblance to her voice. They were the kind of blue often referred to as "cold." But they weren't cold. Deep inside the blue there was a flame, a childish appeal which, at once selfish, self-assured, and completely objective, wanted something from everyone it met.

"The Opera," I said.

"What's so strange about that?" she asked.

"You dream of art, is that it?"

"Yes," she said. "I suppose that's permissible."

She was interested in me. In that *annoyed* kind of way rather common in girls of that age. "Interested" is probably too weak.

"Isn't opera a bit old hat?" I asked. "Padding stuffed into Don Giovanni's leotards, knights arriving on swans, and other knights who kill dragons singing diminished fifths as they expire."

"I sing Mozart," she said.

It was a confession. Now it had become impossible to tease her.

She smelled nice, a faint, somewhat acrid smell, which might have been perfume or perhaps just her own smell. The way I was sitting, I got a glimpse of her bra. It was white. Her neck was very slender.

He, the guy, didn't let go of her. It was quite obvious he was keeping his eye on her while he explained to Picklas how you set up experiments in a synchrocyclotron. An extremely thin metal foil is stretched on a frame and inserted at the spot where the accelerated particles reach their peak velocity. Catastrophes will then occur in this small universe, and the tortured matter gives answers that are captured in bubble chambers. It's called "target preparation."

"Creature discomforts," Picklas said, but I think the remark was wasted on the guy.

He was big and heavy—heavy like a Västmanland farmer. Sure enough, he was from Västmanland, from Köping. There was something sad about that heaviness of his, reminiscent of the way big dogs will sometimes give an impression of sadness.

He spoke with a pronounced Västmanland accent. Every three minutes he looked at Picklas with big astonished eyes when it became evident that Picklas wasn't getting it. Something told me that there was a wide-awake, sharp preparedness under the heavy surface. If someone had tried to hit him—and of course no one in this warm, sunny restaurant, the light still playing in the dust motes between the window curtains, had any ideas along that line—he'd have put his fists up right away.

He wasn't drinking, since he was the one doing the driving. When he got to the coffee, Ann-Marie, too, wanted a brandy with hers.

I was surprised that her name was Ann-Marie. It didn't suit her at all. Ann-Marie was the name of a girl on the same staircase when I was small. I remember there was a lot of fuss

12

one time because I took her doll and hid it. For me, Ann-Marie had to do with tears and childish innocence.

And an angry daddy coming down the stairs to defend his little daughter from me.

So she wanted a brandy while Hasse was looking at his watch. He had an exam at the Tech the next day. You could see he was used to her following him wherever he went, without a lot of questions. But something between them wasn't good.

While we divvied the check, I suggested that they might come along with me to my room to see if I had a bottle of red wine in the shower. (I used to keep red wine in the shower in those days.) He was as bad at divvying the check as most mathematicians are—I insisted on paying for all the drinks, since I had asked them over to our table for a drink. He didn't protest.

I liked him well enough.

"We'll come along for a little while," he said.

We didn't go to my place; it's hard to know why several decades later. We ended up at Imperfect Tense instead. I remember a room with rag rugs and heavy, dusty old furniture and an electric plate on the floor, and I guess we had some more to drink. They were sitting together now, on the couch, and somebody else had joined us.

I was reading from my own poems. Someone had asked me to.

> If the month of June should die,
> the whole world dies.
> A dull smoke rising
> from insipid villages of winter:
> it's the wind that carries it away.
> Silent snow across what once was meadow,
> freedom is in all that carries far away.

Picklas said that this had something in common with Lasse Söderberg's "The Acrobats" and Knaggen that there was something in it of Lars Forssell's "Lettre Sentimentale." I've never been keen on being compared.

I fell silent. I can remember someone making a joke, but I no longer remember just what it was about. At any rate, Knaggen

read—if I remember correctly, he took the book off the shelf—
he didn't like to recite by heart. This was the poem I remembered.

> They know freedom, if freedom
> is a wind that carries far away.
> At night they separate from one another.
> Their shared day is brief.
> At night you see them ride
> the clouds above us.
> None by the other's side.
> No traces. No torches.

Everyone thought it was just incredibly beautiful, except Göran, who thought it was somehow "insincere."

They discussed it for a while without arriving at what Göran
meant by "insincere," and the guy from Royal Tech, Hasse, was
saying, "Now we've got to go" when Ann-Marie—all of them fell
silent when, at long last, she actually said something—asked to
hear my poem once more. I read it slowly and as unpretentiously
as I could manage (it had been praised to the skies in the papers),
and then they left. At the door, she turned around and said to
me:

"We'll see each other again."

It was one of those moments that occur very seldom and which
take hold of you in some strange way.

It was a luminous moment; it was as if everything were encap-
sulated in it.

"Yes," I said. "We'll be seeing each other. Many times."

3

The exercise yard was quite ordinary: a space the size of two
tennis courts, surrounded by very tall chicken wire enclosing two
ancient baobabs, a path of hard-packed red earth, and, in the
middle, somewhat surprisingly, the rear axle of an old truck, half
buried in the ground and overgrown with creepers. To one side,

14

outside the wire, was the half-open shed which housed the prison kitchen. Every day at lunch time a very fat boy ladled sticky rice, which he portioned out into enameled bowls that had been used as washbasins in the morning.

Since it was a jail, the prisoners were evidently exercised one or two at a time; there cannot have been more than three or four of them. The one who always left the exercise yard just as I was brought into it captured my attention.

He was huge, not just fat, but with a big build, dressed in a white mantle and fez; he wore an amulet in the shape of an eagle's claw on a string around his neck. His posture resembled that of a bishop in full pontificals approaching the high altar of some ancient cathedral.

When the gate of red-painted iron pipes opened to let him out and me in, our eyes might well have met; we might have had at least a moment's contact.

But it seemed he simply didn't see me.

Was he blind? Or strange in some other way? Or so far into his own world that no other person meant anything to him anymore?

I was still thinking about him as I sat brooding on my bed around eleven o'clock.

There are meetings that seem objective in some way; you know they mean something without being able to explain, even to yourself, what it is they mean.

Basseré came into my cell half an hour later, oddly surly and rushed.

"Basseré," I said, "what do you know about the governor?"

"He isn't back."

"And when will he be coming back?"

"How am I supposed to know? Not one telephone line to Dakar is working this week."

"I suppose nothing—political—can have happened?"

He had a habit of picking his nose thoughtfully and examining the things he picked from it for a very long time before dispatching them with his middle finger against the inside of his thumb.

"You worry too much. We aren't in Guinea-Bissau. After so many years, you should know that those things don't happen

15

here. Actually, something's been going wrong with the telephone lines all spring. You'll have to talk to that department."

The whole business was rather disturbing, not so much because I thought he was lying about the governor but because I no longer knew where I stood with him. Something about his way of speaking had changed perceptibly from yesterday. I just couldn't put my finger on it.

"You're keeping me under arrest," I said.

"Seems like it."

(He had now made another fascinating discovery in his nose.)

"Wouldn't it be reasonable for me to be made cognizant of an ordinary suspicion, after three days?"

"Under ordinary circumstances," he said.

"What's so extraordinary about me?"

"That's what I'm finding out," he said.

"I can't defend myself against insinuations," I said. "Only against concrete accusations. I come back here after having sailed a couple of tourists to Cape Skiring, something I've been doing for two years, and I am met at the pier by two policemen. Without any kind of explanation. You have to realize that it's getting to be time for me to contact my consul general."

"I'll see that you get pen and paper."

"Another thing," I said. "Who is that big heavy man in the white mantle?"

"Who?"

"The one who goes into the exercise yard ahead of me."

"A confidence man. His name is Amadou M'Bi, and they call him the False Marabout."

"Why?"

"He's been traveling around in three different prefectures, collecting money in the villages from gullible rice farmers."

"On what pretext?"

"The usual one: the Second Coming of the Prophet is imminent. Only those who give their bankbooks to M'Bi the Marabout will survive and enter into glory."

"How do you know that he's a confidence man? Perhaps he believes it himself?"

"I haven't thought that far," Basseré answered. "We've had

16

quite a few religious confidence men in Casamance the last ten years. One was traveling around selling watches: he claimed to be the Great Marabout. Another one sold deliverance from the destruction of the world for twenty francs. One came all the way from Paris and got caught at a car dealer's when he tried to take a car in the name of the district governor. They often have rather intriguing personalities."

"This one seemed unusually intriguing to me."

"I can't let you speak to him."

"Why not?"

"Not the way your case stands at present."

"How does my case stand at present? You haven't even managed to pound out an accusation on your typewriter."

He immediately stopped taking an interest in his nose and started concentrating on his watch instead. It was attached to a wide gold band which circled his wrist.

"I've got something on in Kalonaye. If there are any problems about food or anything like that you should let me know. I'm hoping, just as much as you are, that I'll be able to give you an answer soon."

He closed the door very slowly.

"In that case, get me some cigarettes."

The lock slid into the doorjamb. There was nothing to indicate that he had heard me.

Sometimes I wonder where all those poems I wrote after *River Nights* have gone to. Those I wrote in the spring and summer of 1958, for instance.

I remember that one or two were published in *Femtiotal* and one or two in *Salamander*. There must have been at least twenty of them, and of course they've all disappeared. One that I remember particularly well, because I wrote it the week after my meeting with Hasse and Ann-Marie, was never finished. It was a sonnet, and I can only remember the beginning.

> The fairy of a summer long ago
> was holding some white flowers in her hand.
> Other dreams are shown us from the land
> where the sick Fisher King lies full of woe:

17

Rings are concealed in secret depths below,
sunk through the darkness into bottom sand.
A deep blue sadness we can't understand
spring's sharp light will betimes bestow.

We read a lot of Eliot in Uppsala in those days. But the "sick Fisher King" may have been Hasse.

I know that a whole group of poems were published the following year in some magazine or other, and that they were written up in the arts section of *Morgon-Tidningen*, anyway, and someplace else as well. They were considered more remarkable than anything else I'd done. But I'm almost certain that particular sonnet wasn't included. Probably simply because it wasn't finished.

At least ten days went by without anything happening. I sat in the university's Carolina Library reading American novels from the '30s, sat in Kajsa's Coffee Shop with Nils Elvander and Sven Hamrell, who were going to start a magazine, and I walked back and forth in the English Park a lot. Smoking wasn't allowed in the library. Actually, it was an empty spring. In the park, the snow was still lying in patches under the trees; the paths were wet, almost muddy. There was something relinquished about the sharp spring light.

Every morning between six and seven—I had a hard time sleeping late in the mornings that particular spring—I'd go to Café Uroxen on St. Johannesgatan.

The *slow, imperceptibly advancing decline*, not of memory; no, my memory, faithful as a dog, remains what it always was, but of *feeling*, makes it difficult to return to that time. I can see every scene, both those that were very beautiful and those that were very painful; I can recall events day by day, but when I see them today, everything means something different.

The old events become words in a new language which as yet has hardly had time to be born.

And will it ever be born?

For ten days nothing happened.

On the eleventh, which was a Monday, I came back from Café Uroxen. Some days the gang of chimney sweeps in charge of the chimneys on all of the houses along Öfre Slottsgatan would

18

gather at a particular table around six, having their breakfast. The chimney sweeps in their black coveralls conferred a strange, mythological appearance on the place. I found a note on my door which said, "I looked for you here. I'll be back later. Ann-Marie"—or something along those lines.

It gave me a jolt. It explained to me the peculiar emptiness of the preceding days. I knew it was bound to happen, and I knew that it was the end of my peace that spring. I sat down at the table in the window recess, where the light streamed in, steep and strong, and said goodbye to a lot of years and events.

There was a knock on the door, and she was standing outside, somewhat blonder and more made up than I remembered her, with the kind of tote bag in her hand that people took on trips in those days. And she had on the same gray dress as before.

She looked at me with a hesitant smile.

"I've broken up with Hasse," she said.

My first impulse was to ask her to leave.

"I was sure you would," I said. "Come on in."

She looked around the room. It was in pretty good shape: bookshelves made from boards and bricks, my narrow bed by the north end wall, the desk with its green lamp in the window recess. She put her bag in the entry, came and stood beside me at the window, and looked out on the street.

It had started to rain slightly; you could see the first heavy drops bounce against the black metal roof of Number Ten on the opposite side of the street. There was a light in a window on the first floor. A girl just as blond sat reading a book. I knew her name.

I put my arm around the shoulders of the one called Ann-Marie. There was a strange smell in her hair. It would have seemed acrid if it had been any stronger.

She disengaged herself carefully, and I, fool that I was, thought it might be because she found me too forward.

"Let's go to bed," she said. (Or something like that.) "There's nothing else to do. Let's go to bed."

And she started undoing her dress, which buttoned all the way to the hem. She was wearing the stiff kind of bra common at the time—a lacy construction with stiff edges.

I guess I knew a certain amount about women at that time, but this was something new. Very easy and very hard at the same time. In just a few minutes she had acquired all the initiative, yes, all of reality, and she kept it all, through the afternoon, through the night. I don't believe we got out of the bedclothes, by that time rather tangled, until some time early next morning, and then it was to sneak out together to the bathroom at the end of the hallway. I timed her as she peed. It lasted exactly twenty-one seconds.

I had never known that a woman's orgasms could be so deep and cause such strange and, at the same time, mournful sounds. I was extremely scared, but also completely happy.

Her stomach was just as beautiful, just as strong as I had imagined it under her dress at the City Hotel, ten days before. I was astonished that such a blond girl could have such black and profuse pubic hair. I was tremendously surprised that someone could be so passionately interested in *me*, just as if I'd been carrying a secret message, decipherable by her alone, for which she had been waiting a very long time.

The fear was there as well, and it was a strange feeling of *I'm never going to get out of this.*

"What does music mean to you?" I asked.

"There is something in music that I want to understand," she said. "Something that makes me *hungry*. There's something behind the music that I want to ingest."

"Why did you break up with Hasse?" I asked.

"He drinks such a lot."

"What does Hasse mean to you?"

"A kind of tremendously deep sexual pleasure."

"Really?"

"Yes. It isn't like any other."

I turned quite cold. I got up, jumped into my underpants and trousers, got my shirt on after trying a couple of times to put my head through the sleeve, and threw her underclothes at her: her girdle, her bra, and then her gray dress.

"Here are your clothes. Now leave on the double. Get away from here as fast as you can. I hope you've got a ticket for Stockholm."

She sat up, very surprised.

20

"Yes," I said. "Leave now, right away, before I beat you."

For a moment, sitting there on the edge of the bed, she looked just like the famous girl in Edvard Munch's painting *Puberty.*

"Have you fallen in love with me?" she asked.

Without any sign of triumph, very thoughtfully, almost sadly, that's how she said it.

"I don't know," I said. "Just get out right now. Get out."

I remember that I saw her disappear down the street. She must have brought the raincoat which she worked over her strong, splendid shoulders.

It struck me while I watched her put the raincoat on that the whole time she'd been with me, I hadn't even offered her anything to eat.

4

The next day, which must have been the fourth, I was not alone in the exercise yard. When I was let in through the wire gate by a boyish little policeman, he was already there.

I noticed it right away—it was almost unbelievable that I hadn't noticed the first time.

The false prophet was a hunchback. The hump was very obvious under the white mantle. His gait was unusual, melancholy, bent forward, his hands hidden in the sleeves of his mantle, and with a stubborn, hesitant, perhaps contemplative way of lengthening his stride, all the while muttering something to himself. No doubt that the man was a Wolof, and big even for his people. There was a desolate beauty about the preoccupied manner in which he paced out the exercise yard, apparently blind to everything around him. He walked as if there were something compelling him, leaning forward as if there were an invisible wind he had to overcome.

I caught up with him. He half-turned his face toward me; one of his eyes was splotched with white; he can't have been more than forty, but his eye showed the traces of a disease not uncommon in those regions.

"Hello, my friend," I said.

He didn't answer.

"I haven't seen you here for a few days," I said.

He still didn't answer.

"You don't speak French," I said. "Or else you aren't particularly keen on speaking? I wasn't going to ask you anything personal. You have nothing to fear from me."

He remained silent. Did he imagine that I was some kind of stool pigeon, smuggled in among the prisoners to appropriate their confidences? And why should an ordinary police station in Senegal, with jail attached, employ such subtle Eastern European agents? He strode stubbornly on.

"You mustn't take this the wrong way, my friend," I said. "But I always interpret silence on the part of others as a form of hostility."

The prophet looked up, and for a moment it seemed as if he would even be capable of fixing me with his white, sick, fishlike eye.

"When people are silent I get the feeling that they're trying to annihilate me. That's why I always talk too much."

"You feel that you only exist as long as you're speaking."

I was so surprised that I almost jumped aside. He spoke French with a characteristic Senegalese accent, in a soft, surprisingly low voice.

"Yes," I said. "That's how it is. I defend myself by speaking."

"But all silence is not hostile. The silence of God is not hostile. God's voice is only in the wind, in the stars that are lit at night, but you never hear the voice of God in spoken words. And still God's silence is always a sign that he sees you, that you have his friendship."

"You know, I've never been able to see it that way," I said.

"Silence," said the False Marabout, "is a sign of God."

"Meaning what?"

"That he confidingly entrusts our lives to ourselves. It's up to us to give them meaning."

We walked a few steps in silence. All the while, a bewildered, scrawny hen that looked moth-eaten, was hopping a few steps ahead of us.

"My friend," I said, "I hope you won't take it amiss if I ask you a question that might be considered too personal."

22

"To ask a question is never wrong. To answer it may be a great wrong."

"I have been told that you are a swindler, a False Marabout."

"That is quite correct."

He strode along with the same stubborn gait, so fast and determined that I had a hard time keeping pace with him. And for the first time he added something completely on his own.

"For some people it may be important to be swindlers. In order to keep joy inside of you, it may be necessary to see to it that you are despised by the world."

"You will be sentenced."

"I will be sentenced as soon as the governor returns. And I have reason to believe that the governor will give me a very harsh sentence."

"And you feel no remorse? No fear?"

"Everybody has a unique existence. Remorse and fear belong to most lives."

After that, we exchanged no more words. We walked together in silence, and the shadow of the great baobab moved slowly but surely across the sunlit, dusty yard. When one of the sergeants beat on the old empty gas can at the yard gate to tell us that the exercise period was over, I only had time to say:

"I thank you. It has been instructive for me to talk to you"— something which the false Marabout only answered by still another blind glance from his white, fishlike eye. At the exit not just the duty sergeant but also Monsieur Basseré stood waiting.

"I have news for you that I'm sure will be of interest to you."

"Good or bad?"

"I don't know. News, at any rate. The governor will soon be back. He'll get here any day."

"Are you sure, Monsieur Basseré?"

"Quite sure. You see, I have spoken with him on the phone."

"Oh?"

"He has been notified of your arrest."

"What does he think of it?"

"The governor," said Basseré with a certain dignity, "is not in the habit of discussing particular legal proceedings in such a manner."

"Do I have the right to speak or write to him?"

23

"You will probably be seeing him in the near future."

What was so painful was that actually I did not know what kind of people I had helped across the border to Guinea. I knew that they were not expected to get in, and evidently they had something important to do there. That was all. As far as I could understand, they had no weapons on board my boat. That didn't necessarily mean anything. Weapons may have been waiting for them for years or months in some abandoned house in the forest, or under the mats in some village. The contact had been made by a man in Dakar whom I know quite well, and the pay had been excellent, if only I had got it. It was three times the usual charge for border transport, and in dollars.

I also started to wonder how my boy was managing the store. This boy was actually around forty; his name was Amadou Diop, and he was a combination of first assistant, chauffeur, and accountant in the small grocery store I'd started in Ziguinchor four years earlier. What sold best were goods for European tourists and wooden sculpture more authentic than the incredible junk sold at the local handicrafts fair.

Suppose Amadou knew more than I did about what was going to happen to me—what would he do with the store? Would he remain faithful and only skim some off the top, or would he fleece me completely?

I was getting the feeling that my four years in Ziguinchor were now rapidly coming to an end. And I didn't know what that end would be like. If it had happened on the other side of the river, I would have been dead four or five days now anyway, and wouldn't have had to worry about the grocery store, where the kith and kin of my First Assistant had no doubt plundered the shelves long ago, while he himself had taken charge of the cash.

5

A few days later—I mean *then*, in 1958—I took the train down to Stockholm. This was not to see Ann-Marie but to participate in a poetry reading at Petra's Salon in the south part of Stockholm. Petra was a nice, very artistic, very motherly gallery owner who used to invite poets, young poets in particular, to read in her gallery.

It was one of those perfectly blue spring evenings, with a lot of red in the sunset; one after the other, I saw the Cathedral, the barracks of the Royal Uppland Regiment, and the Sture Monument up on Kronåsen sink into the redness.

The train—I remember it as a dollhouse—had just a few passengers: a couple of girls in light-colored skirts with wide fabric belts and two university teachers who discussed the pension reform. The evening light came hesitantly through the vibrating, not quite clear contents of a water pitcher, in which the particles, viewed from a certain angle, appeared like a shimmering sky full of stars.

It was the kind of evening when everything spells farewell. Somewhere around Märsta I started to experience a strange, itching sensation deep inside my lower right jaw, as if a very small thunderstorm were happening there.

I've always construed such things as warnings, often without knowing what they were warning me of: changes in the subtle field of force surrounding us, the signal that tells us we are about to be vanquished, that we wish for more than is possible to obtain.

I sat down to think over my situation in a corner of the railway carriage, where the sun no longer shone as strongly.

To start with there was my poetry, which at the moment gave me a certain renown, and which might also procure me a fellowship or two. At that time, poets didn't live on their poetry but by writing newspaper articles, an opportunity they had because they were poets. But I didn't want to write newspaper articles, and perhaps I wasn't able to, anyway.

Would I go on for the rest of my life writing thin little books of poetry that good reviews in *Morgon-Tidningen*, *Aftonbladet*, and *Expressen*, hoping to get a fellowship around Christmas time? How many thin little poetry books would I be able to produce?

Then it was the thesis I was doing for Professor Svanberg, which had been lying fallow for two years. I'd catch sight of it from time to time, the way you might catch sight of an old acquaintance in the street: an awful lot of folders in the far corner of the bookcase, a card index consisting of a few hundred quotations that did not want to come together, and some worried letters from my professor, in his clear, flowing hand, letters which always started, "Brother!"

What is open to a literary historian? The long, compromising road to a professor's chair? Or the much more probable road: becoming a teacher in some high school? It wasn't that long ago since I'd had teachers like that myself. Some of them, too, had published thin little books of poetry.

What else was there? Yes, what was there in this world?

My background, my native spot, my starting-point into the world, was a four-room apartment in the south part of Stockholm, where I had spent my school years with my parents and my sister, who graduated a bit before me. Neither of us ever troubled about our home or our parents. Papa worked for the Gas Company, and, for the first few years in the '50s, Mama worked as a cashier at the co-op store across the street. My sister and I were good students, '50s' fashion, with scholarships and essay prizes and good grades. Nobody expected anything different.

My sister was the first one in the family to graduate from a gymnasium, and I was the second. Nobody in the family was quite sure how to celebrate this, but everyone was very proud.

In this four-room milieu, with my sister's piano practice (in the candlesticks over the piano, the kind of yellow spiral candles popular at the time), Papa hunched over the radio, pictures Uncle Stig had made with wooden matches hanging on the walls, I developed—in a totally serene, totally harmonious manner—into a poet.

Hölderlin and Rilke, Eliot and Pound: I absorbed everything unself-consciously; it somehow formed a part of the atmosphere of the apartment just like the spiral candles did, in their own way. Harmoniously and serenely, I grew into not Western culture (because I didn't know it) but into a dream of Western culture. In the same way, some of my contemporaries grew into a dream of the Motorcycle or a dream of the soccer team making the All-Sweden finals at Råsunda.

This dream of mine proved useful. It could be filled in indefinitely.

(Should some of us be blamed for having found dreams that could be filled in or others for never finding them?)

And no exit from it.

There were mostly young people in Petra's studio, young, friendly faces that now, night fallen at last, seemed to exude warmth. Or was it all the candle flames in Petra's studio, flickering precariously in Chianti bottles, that is to say from the necks of Chianti bottles, that created this warm, attentive light, as in a Georges de La Tour?

I was the third one to read. Paul Andersson had promised to come but had reneged at the last moment; the readers ahead of me were a rather shy, gawky guy called Jahnson, who read from something called *Fairy Tales from Court*, and a poet with beautiful dark hair and an evangelical background, who had written something about the National Railroad and what it feels like to put your ear against the track and hear a train far in the distance.

I don't know whether it was me they had come to hear, but there was a different kind of silence in the room. I read:

> Oh these soft waves of grass, Euridyce,
> this other wave of softness,
> resembling neither sea nor verdigris.

In the last row, on folding chairs, were Hasse and Ann-Marie, of course. It was some time before I discovered them in the dark, in the Chianti-bottle light. But there they sat, actually. And it felt like security of a kind.

Sometimes, especially a bit later on in the early '60s, it was usual to have a little discussion, some questions about the meaning of the poem and about the poetry of commitment, that sort of thing. But it wasn't yet the custom in the spring of 1958, at least not in Petra's Salon.

It almost seemed as if they were taking a parental pride in me. Not a word about what had happened the last time. Ann-Marie looked somewhat more tired, her face made up a bit.

"Let's go down to Zum, or someplace like that," Hasse said.

"Zum is a madhouse," I said. "Let's hit Mosebacke instead."

"Fantastic poetry," Hasse said. "I haven't read that much poetry, since I'm a physicist, but I sure thought that last one was great."

"Like sunset on black velvet. Sunset, viewed from an airplane when it's already dark down below but the sunlight is still on the clouds. It's like that in a couple of places in Mozart's *Requiem*."

"Have you flown?" I asked.

"Yes, I just did. I was invited down to Göteborg to audition at Stora Teatern. They need a Susanna."

"Fantastic. Have you got a chance?"

"Don't know."

"You look tired?"

"Nothing strange about that. I've had a little trouble with Hasse."

(Somehow Hasse had gotten behind us as we were walking down Hornsgatan.)

"What do you want from him?"

"I don't know."

"Can't you see how weak he is?"

"But that may be the thing that I need in him."

As I remember her through all the years, across the seas, across the continents, in the piss-smelling tepid African winter night in the District Jail in Ziguinchor, she had two attributes.

One was a strong attraction. No joke: the kind that can actually drive you mad. The other was a fragility, a side that was turned away, that didn't want to have anything to do with men or with people in general: there was something in her that reminded me of the shabby suburban woods of the '40s and the early '50s, land that had recently been real woods but which was now being invaded by its proximity to apartment houses, and which was becoming something no longer either woods or not-woods: worn paths, shiny carpets of needles under the trees whose branches were disfigured by the little huts that the children made with materials from the building sites. A woods whose skating pond was being drained, whose wild rabbits had been replaced by tame ones in cages that were often plundered by strange old men late at night, or—still worse—were crucified alive against a fence.

A suburban woods with discarded rubbers, ladies' underwear glimpsed in the bushes, a pair of underpants that might derive from the latest sex murder or from peaceful moonlight walk a male and female bus conductor had taken between runs: that's what she felt like.

And what wouldn't I have given to possess her in that kind of suburban woods, to push her up against one of the worn climbing trees and let my hand slide inside the waistband of her skirt, the panty girdle with its more tensile resistance, and then to deprive her of the thing that was personal to her and still not personal. At the risk of any moment being surprised by some curious and malicious gang of teenage boys.

In the '50s, when she still got some really big parts and was one of the great, promising young talents, I think many people who heard her sing must have been attracted by something along that line, without of course being aware of it. In the last analysis, the critics reacted more to something they felt than to something they heard. Something boyish and yet not boyish, turned away yet not turned away, present and yet not present.

In short: when they heard her sing, their own existence acquired doubleness and depth; in some subtle way they were reminded that everyone is a citizen of two worlds at the same time.

Success came quickly for her then, and even today it is hard to understand why there weren't more and bigger successes. They started coming, and they stopped as quickly as they'd come.

That evening, they had hardly even started.

2   Faust in Malmö 1958

1

"Monsieur Basseré," I said, the next time he came on his cautiously amiable tour of inspection, "Monsieur Basseré, is it possible that you know what's going on with the governor?"

"There is every indication that he is on his way here. And that is not all. The news on the radio indicates that political events are coming to a head. Troops have entered Gambia in order to prevent a Soviet-initiated coup."

"Our troops?"

"Oh, I really appreciate the fact that you put it *that* way, my dear Jan; yes, it's our troops who have entered Gambia."

"My dear Basseré, from the window of my cell I can see the sky getting grayer every day. The rains are coming."

"Jan, I will arrange for you to take longer walks."

"That is very nice of you, Monsieur Basseré, but that isn't really what I was getting at."

"Oh?"

"What I wanted to say is that the roads will soon be impassable."

"But, my dear Jan, the governor, who is the only one able to prove your innocence, does not need to use the roads. He has access to an airplane."

"That's quite true; if, that is, he is allowed to fly."

"Why shouldn't he be?"

"Man proposes, God disposes, Monsieur Basseré."

"'Who should know that better than I, an old police chief in a Moslem district?"

"Monsieur Basseré, before I get out of here they'll have robbed my store right down to the shelves. By the time I get my sailboat away from the police who took custody of it, there won't be much left of it. In short, Monsieur Basseré, you've got to understand that I'm getting somewhat impatient."

"I am sure that no one will violate your rights in any way. As long as I am the prefect, no one will touch your property."

"Are you sure of that?"

"Remember, Jan, that once upon a time you actually saved me from a catastrophe."

"But that's such a long time ago. I only remember it vaguely."

"But I haven't forgotten."

"Basseré," I said, "if we're still friends, how could you claim the other day that the governor was actually on his way, when evidently you and all the other free people knew that he was *not*. Please explain that to me if you will."

"No one," Monsieur Basseré said, "no one at all, except the Creator himself, is omniscient."

With that, he concluded his morning visit.

Later the same day, to my surprise, I was joined in the exercise yard by the false prophet Amadou M'Bi.

"I am starting to feel anxiety and despair," I said. "I don't know how much longer I will be able to hold on to my peace of mind."

"But for a long time you have only succeeded in doing so by opening a door to the past," said M'Bi, gravely.

"I'm not quite sure how long that trick will work," I said.

"If it works," said M'Bi, "then it's no trick. When you're there, then you're there in actuality."

"I can't always get those doors open," I said. "Can you?"

"Of course not," said M'Bi, turning his great, white, blind eyeball toward me as if he were able to see, in spite of everything, right through the china-colored membrane. "Of course not. Also, I have memories so terrible that I'd never dare touch them."

He seemed to be on his way into his usual silence, and I was about to accept it for a fact, when once again he turned to me and said, the way you speak comfortingly to a small child:

"Anyway it'll all be much better in the morning."

"How do you know that?"

"The governor will be back tomorrow."

"But how do you know?"

"The chickens told the goats next to us here. Can't you hear them cackling all the time?"

34

2

Her face, pure, clear, unexpected, with that amazing ability to lie which only some very naked faces possess—strangely enough, her face is the thing that's most difficult to remember.

My clearest image of it may be from *Faust* in Malmö the fall of 1958. How did we get there? I don't remember much from the summer in between, or do I?

Hasse had an invitation to go somewhere, perhaps Geneva or Amsterdam; at any rate it was very important for his education. Of course he knew that if he went I'd still be there. All summer. And she'd be left in Stockholm. They'd promised her a small part at the Drottningholm Theater, something in a Rossini production if I remember correctly. The question, of course, was what would happen. Would I move to Stockholm from Uppsala for the summer? And was it something I could handle? And, when all was said and done, was Hasse happy to be going away?

Her face, pure, clear, and unexpected, but also lying. I've never really seen anything like it. Blond, with finely cut, full lips, beautiful features, but an offended kind of face, the kind you often see in film stars, who seem terribly worried that we won't see them and, at the same time, deeply insulted if we really see them for a moment. A little girl, disappointed in life once and for all, or once and for all disappointed in her expectations of life.

It was quite possible that he really wanted me to free him from her, wanted me to move down to Stockholm, sleep with her most of the afternoon and all night, and force my more complex poet's nature on her, the way he imagined that nature to be. Then at last he'd be free from demands that, anyhow, were too great.

Actually the whole landscape (which I always imagined as a forest landscape: tall sandy ridges, dry soil, the scent of sharp little pine needles, heavy boulders smelling of heated rock) was completely foreign to me. At the end of the '50s, I was living totally enclosed in my dream. Even these people were dreamed. Perhaps it was best that way.

Neither one of us was able to stay with her that night, since

35

both of us wanted to just as much. Hasse wanted me to stay at his place, but I didn't want that either, so the upshot was that around one in the morning I ended up in the very smallest room, a kind of closet behind the front desk, in the Salvation Army hotel on Drottninggatan. The spring night already gleamed white through the window when I went to bed, and I had a crawling pain or chill, rather like the feeling you get when you've exhausted your last inner resources.

I went back home to Uppsala the next day, on the slow, melancholy kind of train they had in the '50s. The strange thing is that I stayed in Uppsala all summer while she was alone in Stockholm.

The city had that kind of quality: it could hold on to you. It wasn't the famous jackdaws around the spire of the Cathedral, nor the ugly brown river. But there was something which made it possible to get entangled in your own dreams. The heavy, green shade under the deciduous trees that were still standing on Skolgatan. The subdued murmur of the English Park. The smell of not particularly innovative sauces from the Delmonico dining hall. I tackled my paper once more, started getting up early in the morning and going to the Carolina Library to read Baroque poetry. The summer of 1958 was nice and warm, with rain sometimes at night. Hot, friendly days when the light plunged into my deep well of a yard on the other side of Slottsgatan.

I wrote very little poetry that summer. Most of what I wrote were fragmentary four-liners, almost always concerned with my persistent, strange feeling of *absence*. If I remember right, one of them went something like this:

> In the shadow, this single one of all the colors
> turns into mine, concerns my destiny the most.
> When the wind flings opens the window of the day,
> then the thing I'd keep is gone already.

That summer, I was in the habit of having lunch at Café Alma in the university cellars, a very simple lunch, just a cup of coffee and a liverwurst sandwich with pickles. (Good Lord, when did I last eat a liverwurst sandwich with pickles?) The daily papers were there, and each day I looked eagerly for the Rossini at the Drottningholm Theater.

It must have been either too late or too early: I found no trace of her. Articles by Tingsten and Lagercrantz, debates about sincerity in poetry and other topics which seemed important at the time. Sometimes I felt proud when I was quoted. I still wasn't quite used to being a poet, to being one of the best, to being taken seriously. I hadn't even quite gotten used to people taking poetry seriously.

In short: the days passed, quietly. I even made contact with a pleasant, rather too tall, blond, or reddish-blond, woman whom I met at Domtrappkällaren with a friend of hers. I expected a lot from her. She was so lively, so obviously interested. I was, so to speak, on the way out of my destiny, on the way to avoiding it (just like the entire Swedish '50s seemed on its way out of its own destiny then, almost managing to avoid it) when suddenly it's August already and Ann-Marie calls me one day.

"Hi there," I said.

"Hi. We never got together last summer."

"But summer isn't over."

"Do you think so? It is, for me."

"How was Drottningholm?"

"You never came to hear me."

"I'm sorry. Somehow, I got stuck in Uppsala."

"Do you *want* to get together? Do you really want to?"

"I think so."

(That's the way we spoke in those days. It's easy to forget that those people I'm speaking of were just past twenty at their time in the story.)

"How about Hasse?"

"Hasse has been in Switzerland all the time with some— accelerator they're testing. We could have seen each other without him getting hurt."

"I don't think you quite understand me. I'd like to see you without you worrying at all about what Hasse will say."

"Couldn't you have said so a bit sooner?"

"Why?"

"Because if you had, this summer might have been less of total loss."

This was a kind of turning point, because after that conversation I got into the habit, the rather expensive habit as far as that's concerned, of calling her every night after the performance, to ask how it went, whether the Great Conductor had tried to flirt with her again, if the audience was the same, hopeless snobs, like the night before. One night there was a state visit with Social-Democratic ministers who clapped in the wrong place and a head of state from some African country who didn't understand anything at all and who spoke loudly with his secretaries and assistants in the middle of a *recitativo secco*, until one of the best basses at the Opera simply roared at him, "Now you'll have to shut up, dammit, if we're going to have an opera here."

It was a wonderful world, totally strange to me, and meeting it through her merry, coolly flowing telephone conversations made me happy.

I don't know why, but right then I didn't need anything else. Perhaps I was still busy dreaming about her.

Of course we were always saying that I'd have to come down and hear her before the season was over.

But it was in Malmö that we saw each other. Ingmar Bergman—who at that time was simply the director of the Malmö City Theater, and, together with another half-dozen young directors, was considered promising—had his first great success in the middle of October with a production of Goethe's *Faust*, with Max von Sydow as Faust and Toivo Pawlo as Mephistopheles. The word spread fast: everyone, as the saying goes, had to see it. One day *Vecko-Journalen* calls to ask if I want to write something about it. Their theater critic had been there, but evidently they aren't quite satisfied; they want something additional, perhaps the atmosphere around the performance. I call Ann-Marie to ask if she'd like to come with me. She'd love to, but she won't be able to come until the next day. She has to go to the first of her voice lessons. We talk back and forth, finally deciding that we'll meet at the theater; we'll stay at the Hotel Kramer, but in separate rooms, in order "not to feel any kind of pressure." The next day, after I've arranged for tickets and got a berth in a sleeper to Malmö, she calls up and says that no way will it work.

"Then the hell with you," I say.

And I leave.

After spending the afternoon walking on strange, flat, open streets along canals of a kind that were completely foreign to me at the time (then, and actually throughout my life, the woods are where I am at home) I arrive at the theater.

Among the women around the well in Act One is Bibi Andersson, then still very young. Her rippling laughter rises above the others'. Toivo Pawlo, the Mephistopheles in this performance, has a muted fall at the end of his sentences: the tired assurance of someone who's heard it all before, not once, but many times.

Next to me is the empty seat Ann-Marie should have occupied.

In that tired devil's voice is the whole of the '50s. It says goodbye to everything it wanted and wasn't able to realize. The small Sweden of that time, still idyllic, on a journey away from its own possibilities, journeying toward the gray, stern, co-operative fortress that the '60s and '70s would erect on the land of the old allotment gardens. Already in the tired devil's voice was the autumnal wind which would once and for all disperse the short summer of fantasy that was my moment. We didn't know it. Not yet.

Act One was an undoubted success. The applause flowed to greet the actors: this was one of the great evenings that would go down in the history of the theater. A little giddy, I strolled about the handsome lobby, modernistic after the manner of the '50s, looking more inside myself than outward. At the last moment before the bell rings, I discover, behind the backs of some solid Malmö inhabitants, Ann-Marie and Hasse. He has his arm around her back, where her hair has grown a lot longer. She looks up at him. Should I pretend that I haven't seen them? The question is no longer pertinent, because they steer straight for me.

"Hi. I had a seat for you."

"I know. I'm sorry. But Hasse got in touch so late that I never had a chance to speak to you."

"It doesn't matter. I'm already used to your lying. It's your way of keeping control over other people."

Hasse looked a bit embarrassed. I couldn't see why. But evidently there was something about the situation, perhaps the unmanliness of sheltering behind a woman's lies, which made him feel uncomfortable.

"Hi," I said.

"Hi," he said.

"You're passing through again, sort of?"

"I'm going back to Geneva on Monday. I was in Oslo. It was kind of easy to stop in here on my way."

"I can see that," I said. "But Ann-Marie might have told me. It would've saved her a lot of trouble."

The bell rang for the next act, and we returned to our separate seats. They were someplace far in back of me, and I didn't have the slightest desire to turn around to look at them.

During Act Three, in a manner characteristic of her, Ann-Marie came along and sat down next to me. She simply took hold of my hand, bit it and carefully put it back in my lap, rather as if it were something I'd lent her. I didn't particularly feel like talking to her.

"Now," she said. "Now I'm come back to you for good."

"What about Hasse?" I asked.

"I'm through with him. We're through with each other."

"Did you have to bring him to the theater then?"

"Don't ask me. That's just how it worked out."

That night, for the first time, I noticed a strange weariness in her voice. As if nothing would really be able to interest her any longer, as if life was basically something she performed in.

I took her to my hotel, and believe it or not, the only thing I did was to put her to bed. I sat beside her for a long time and watched her sleep, peaceful as a little child, and I didn't understand a thing about either her or myself. I thought:

"It's within my power to either destroy or save this person."

And neither was something I really wanted to do.

After that we had some good days. We were lucky in the weather, which suddenly changed to become warm and midsummery. We went to Hälsingborg, where the Hälsingborg Exposition had taken place a few years before, light and optimistic, out on the so-called Parapet. We walked on this breakwater or pier toward the Sound, watched the ships moving up or down under their solemn smoke, the sailboats dancing around in the slight fall gusts, the ramparts in Helsingör, and perhaps—although I'm not sure you can actually see it—a yellow dot which Ann-Marie insisted was the Swedish writer Hjalmar Söderberg's yellow house on the opposite shore.

The whole world on the opposite shore. And for a moment, anyway, I experienced a ferocious desire to get away, to other seas, other shores, and other voices, a desire that was much stronger than my desire for the strong, compact body that clung closely to mine.

We took a trip to Copenhagen, drank beer among all the hitch-hiking Dutch and Germans at Hovedbanegaarden, found our way into the area behind the Town Hall, and ended up at the small Café Tokanten by the fountain on the other side.

Yes, I think it was a happy day. Everything was in balance, all our problems were unsolved, there was a threat around every corner, and time, swift as a waterfall, or perhaps as a waste pipe in the brown wallpapered wall of some dubious hotel, rushed on. Just the two of us, completely happy.

I don't know how many times or how long I slept with her that night. I only remember that I went to sleep in her arms and that the sound of rushing water woke me, far off in the darkness.

And I no longer knew my name.

We were supposed to see more of each other that fall, but two things intervened. One had to do with me, and the funny thing is, I can't for the life of me remember what it was. It was something important, and it happened to me. That's all I know. Perhaps I'll tell the story some other time.

I was back in Uppsala by the end of October when a friend of hers, I think from the Opera School, called to say that Ann-Marie was very sick, that she'd just been taken to the Caroline Hospital.

"An accident?"

"No, not at all. A virus of some kind, one of those they don't know much about. She's weak. She wants you to come see her."

I remember that I did, not just once but several times. I remember her as very thin. They hadn't got the better of her illness. Her head was cradled on her arm, and her temple had the color of thin china.

I remember lying down beside her on the blue hospital blanket. She put her arms around me, and her fear of death made everything terrifying and meaningless. October turned into November, the leaves outside the window were fewer, and soon snow was falling everywhere.

What I can't remember is whether she died that winter or whether she survived.

3

"Monsieur Basseré, why are you banging so heavily on my cell door? Basseré, what the hell do you want in the middle of the night?"

"It isn't Monsieur Basseré, it's Sergeant Baldë."

"In the middle of the night?"

"It isn't the middle of the night, it's five in the morning."

"But my dear Sergeant, why are you throwing in my ordinary clothes? You haven't come to announce my execution?"

"We're not in the habit of executing prisoners in Senegal, Monsieur. Least of all without due procedure. But you're supposed to get dressed, because an important personage who is short of time wants to see you at six o'clock."

"Good Lord, you don't mean to say that the governor has returned?"

"His Excellency the Governor of Casamance Basse returned on the regularly scheduled flight last night."

"Could you get me some hot water for shaving?"

"I'll see if there's any room on the stove. But, as I said, time is short. Monsieur Basseré has decided that I am to drive you in the jeep belonging to the International Children's Emergency Fund."

"What time does it get light?" (It was the first time in ten, perhaps fifteen days that I was interested in questions of daylight and hours. All the clocks in the world started up again. Some of them with the slow, heavy ticktock sound of serious tower clocks, some with the ticking of nervous little pocket watches, and some with the silent, frenetic conviction of modern digital clocks. But all of them were going down the same river.)

"Much later," Sergeant Baldë said. "Not until seven o'clock, this time of year. We've got to start in the dark."

"Are we going far?"

"I don't know, Monsieur Bohman. I haven't received my orders yet."

"Sergeant Baldë, why did you have such a hard time waking me up today? I'm usually a very light sleeper. You seem to have made quite a racket this morning."

"It's true, Monsieur Bohman, I even hit the cell door with a cast-iron stool without waking you. The other prisoners were quite alarmed."

"Perhaps we sometimes have to make ourselves insensitive to certain things in order to become more sensitive to others."

It was the same jeep I had ridden in before; it carried traces (in the shape of flaking letters on its sides and on the radiator) of having at some time belonged to UNICEF. It started easily, and the chickens in the yard, who had learned from experience, threw themselves aside, away from the beams of the headlights the moment they were turned on. At the last second, just before the guard opened the gate, Monsieur Basseré came running up with two plastic bags, which he quickly handed to the sergeant. For a moment it occurred to me that of course the bags *might* contain my things. But in that case, they ought to have been bigger and bunchier. I *had* had a jacket when I came.

Basseré looked up at me with friendly, sleepy eyes.

"My dear Jan, it's been a pleasure, as always, to have dealings with you. I hope you will overlook the fact that we haven't been able to do much to ensure your comfort."

"You mean this is the end of my arrest?"

"Everything points that way."

"Good-bye then, Monsieur Basseré. But won't we see each other soon in my shop?"

43

"That's hard to say, Monsieur Bohman."

The wheels shrieked on the curve as we passed through the gate, and the sergeant, who evidently had never been a very good driver, barely avoided running into a group of white-clad women, on their way from one place to another, some with half-naked babies sitting in enamel basins balanced on top of their heads, some with rice in their basins.

When we drove through the archway to the governor's residence, dawn had arrived, even though the light was still faint, and I realized that (in all probability) I was saved.

Most of the men in the archway were still asleep. The beggars rolled up in their brown shrouds, the black-coated scribes with their heads buried in their collars. In the courtyard motorcycle orderlies and drivers were already standing around in a talking, smoking group, some holding steaming coffee cups. The same strange mixture of marketplace and Roman camp as in other places in Senegal. A very tall Serer, whom I had never seen before, received us and conducted us up the endless, cracked marble steps into which lizards would disappear on beautiful summer days.

Soon we were inside the complicated system of blue-green passages. Warm green light streamed from the radio operator's room. A darkened aquarium, lit by the natural daylight coming through a window, peopled by nervous crickets. Through the panes I saw the sun come up.

Next thing, we were in front of the governor. Immense in his white mantle, sitting at his desk, he did not give us even a moment of his attention. He seemed completely absorbed by something else, namely getting someone on the telephone, a solid, old-fashioned French crank-up set sitting among the files and stacks of paper on the desk. He turned the handle and roared at the operators with the deep, dull roar of a lion. It was obvious that he was speaking to someone in Dakar and that he kept losing the connection due to technical difficulties.

During one of his most furious outbursts at the exchange, whether it was the one in Ziguinchor or the one in Dakar, or possibly some exchange in the infinity of forest and dry savannah between us and Dakar, our eyes happened to meet.

44

He looked straight into my eyes with a kind of bitter exhilaration, a mixture of humor, antipathy, and tenderness, perhaps with the tolerance of a wise person for a stupider one, which sent a shudder through me. In the years I'd lived in Casamance, I'd never believed the provincial governor was a man to trifle with— he had always impressed me when, from time to time, we'd met at various functions. Never, however, had he been more frightening than today. He even appeared physically larger, an effect that might owe something to the morning light from the window behind him. With a single gesture of his wide-sleeved right arm, he emptied the room of policemen and assistants.

"My dear Monsieur Bohman, you're causing me grief and certain problems."

"Your Excellency, you know that I am a simple storekeeper doing some sailing on the river. Now that has suddenly come to be viewed as a criminal activity."

"Criminal, is it? Who has said that it is criminal to carry a few tourists on the river? Not me, at any rate."

"But Your Excellency, why then do you keep me under arrest in a jail in the Ziguinchor Prefecture?"

"Because before God we are all sinners, my dear Jan."

"But in that case, Your Excellency, not all sinners are punished equally, and not all are kept under arrest by the Prefect Basseré in Ziguinchor with equal justification."

"That's quite true, Monsieur Bohman. Different people receive very different rewards for their deeds. In the long run, you will be rewarded for yours. But not now. And not here. Monsieur, I have to ask you to leave Senegal within forty-eight hours. You have caused a serious incident with a friendly neighboring country."

"Your Excellency, this means economic ruin for me. My boat, my store . . . And besides, there's nowhere for me to go."

"Nonsense, my dear friend. You have an excellent assistant who, I am sure, will be able to borrow sufficient money to buy both the boat and the store."

You eventually reach an age where the main features of your life already seem determined. As in the classic inferno of nineteenth-century physics, where billiard balls, once their mass, direction, and power are givens, cannot end up anywhere but in the pockets where they do end up, you are, so to speak, help-lessly entangled in the web of components and resultants, and you see yourself as a ball rolling toward a grave in the far corner of the green table.

You have, once and for all, thoroughly neglected the life intended for you at home in Sweden—I can't help wondering what it would have looked like. More poetry books perhaps, lots of poems, and lots of empty wine bottles, too. Perhaps I'd have lived in a house in a Stockholm suburb and been on fellowship committees and belonged to impressive associations and written articles on poetry in *Stockholms-Tidningen* or *Morgon-Tidningen*. Or perhaps I'd already have been lying in the Maria Cemetery, dead before my time from red wine and amphetamines.

But neither thing happened. Instead of being a member of the Swedish Academy, I had become a storekeeper in Africa, dealing in this and that, not without occasional success. Of course it spelled failure. On the other hand there were pluses that balanced the minuses: I was alive. While the governor continued slapping his hands together in a strange gesture, as if he were applauding his own thoughts, looking up at the ceiling, where the rotating fan looked as if it kept chasing its own shadow, I began to realize that the time had now come for another big surprise. This fan and its shadow were also clocks measuring time.

If it became known that I had to leave the country my boat and my store wouldn't be expensive buys. What hadn't been stolen already wouldn't come to more than a few thousand francs. "Of course," I almost said to myself—the thought put me in a good mood. I was getting out of the game of pocket billiards: the ball refused to roll the way the cue had intended.

I've always been like that.

It was the same when I left Sweden in the spring of 1961 and went to Lyon. I refused to become a poet, because I could already see where it would lead.

"This is the end of me as a businessman, I'm sure you realize that, Your Excellency," I said. "What Amadou hasn't stolen, no one will pay a cent for. I am a ruined man."

The governor lifted his shoulders slightly.

We had enough of a past in common so that he might easily hate me.

Simultaneously, it occurred to me that this was a Swedish thought. In Sweden, sour old hate-relationships played a peculiarly large part, especially in academic and bureaucratic circles. The Senegalese have hardly any talent for hate. Perhaps it's because they're more religious. You might annihilate your enemies or you might forgive them, but hating them is almost inconceivable. For a Diola, raised almost without exception in the forest, with a deeply loyal way of life, hate is probably a feeling that's much too self-centered.

I wonder, by the way, whether Hasse still hates me?

"My dear friend," the governor said. "I fear you have to regard your boat and your store as lost. This is the price of the game you were playing. Where are you going?"

"The same way back, I guess. To Lyon. Possibly to Paris. I don't think Sweden has much to offer."

4

I haven't been in Sweden since 1962.

Then it was in the middle of winter and just for three days, to have lunch with some people who wanted to see if I could help them manufacture plastic pipes in the Free Trade Zone outside Dakar. I advised them against the project, they went ahead anyway and have since made scads of money. Koch, the consul in Dakar, complains about the terrible taxes. I don't recall that we used to complain about taxes in the '50s. Or maybe people did?

From the '40s until the mid-'50s, we lived on Heleneborgsgatan in one of those large, rather dark buildings, until my father finally managed to buy a row house in Ängby.

He was only a meter reader for the gas company. He died in 1957, two years after he'd got the row house finished. I don't know that his death touched me all that much. I didn't dare deal with it in earnest. There was something hidden in his life that could have made me very unhappy, so deeply unhappy that I'd never have found my way out again.

I remember his evenings in the '50s. Home around seven, in the cold, damp winter on Riddarfjärden; have something to eat; talk to Mama and my sister about how she'd done in school. (She was always the one who had the task of doing well; he must have been disappointed when she married, so soon after graduating, a common baker and became a housewife. He'd always expected her to become something "great." And he wasn't impressed, either, when Hjalle opened his own bakery on Långholmsgatan. Papa started to expect something "great" from me, instead.)

Then he used to sit next to the radio, listening. Accordion music and symphonies. Debates and the pension issue and Sweden's relationship to the Western Allies, the entertainment program *Merry-Go-Round* with Lennart Hyland, and evening prayer; he absorbed it all, and everything seemed to stay inside him.

This listening to the radio was something he'd brought with him from the clayey, flat land in Nibble, in the Hallstahammar district, where he'd grown up. He'd lived alone with a very old mother—she had given birth to him when she herself was in her forties—all through his teens and his twenties. There was a melancholy in him which somehow was connected with his own fatherlessness, a weight or wordlessness. It didn't in any way prevent him from being rather voluble. When he played bridge and drank schnapps with Mama's brothers (two of them lived in the south part of Stockholm during the '50s, one right next to us, on Högalidsgatan, the other down by Hammarby Harbor, on the second floor of an old white wooden house, together with a wife whom I never actually spoke to, because she never visited us) he would become almost boisterous.

There were a lot of things about my parents and their friends that were completely foreign to me and which today I can't even explain.

None of them had any kind of importance or prestige in the society they lived in. Still, they were extremely careful about differences in social levels so microscopic that no one I meet today, not even in the jungles of Casamance, would notice them.

Uncle Stig, for example, was an accountant at United Laundry. It was extremely important not just that he was an accountant but also that he wasn't the "chief accountant." My father "cooperated with the gas company."

There was no topic of conversation that could inspire my parents and their friends as strongly as the misfortunes of others. Somehow, other people's failures, calamities, and weaknesses were one giant battery from which they drew their own vitality. At that time, the late '50s, Stockholm's evening papers started to understand their audience, filling columns with exactly the kind of conversation the people of that class carried on. The subject was always the incomprehensible, totally astonishing, generally unbelievable mishaps which might happen to anybody, any time. Someone might park his car so unfortunately that the hand brake slipped and the car rolled over a pair of twins in a baby carriage; someone might get up at three in the morning with an irritating cough after his latest winter cold and, instead of the intended bottle of cough medicine, take a big tablespoon of ammonia and be found dead on the kitchen floor by his wife the next morning.

Not only did this kind of fantasy have a hold in the fear that exists in everyone and, in particular, among little people—it put them in a good mood.

It had something to do with their deep conviction that everything *had to be paid for.* I remember at the University, at a graduate seminar, I had an entertaining discussion with Professor Victor Svanberg concerning Linnaeus' *Nemesis Divina.* Svanberg wanted to see the strange work of Linnaeus' old age as derived from all kinds of biblical and classical sources: he spoke of Oedipus and the Book of Job. I almost caused a scandal in his seminar by pointing out that the moral of *Nemisis Divina* is exactly the moral of the lower middle class, not only what they say but also—which is rare—what they do. If a window is opened, another window always has to be closed. If someone wins the lottery, he'll probably develop lung cancer next year. On the other hand, you haven't won the lottery this week, you can always tell yourself that in all probability neither will you this week get lung cancer. There is balance in reality, says Linnaeus and his eminent eighteenth-century friends, a harmony or, if you like, an economy that operates even when we cannot immediately discern it.

"That's it, that's it exactly," says the old lady in the tobacco shop who sells lottery tickets and keeps the coffee pot going all day in the little room behind the curtain where she takes her breaks, "that's exactly the way I imagine the world to be."

Even then I must have had the feeling that they were all wrong. There is no balance. There's nothing to say that virtue will prove more successful than vice.

Isn't it stupid, having to point out something like that? A single walk through the market on the Medina in Dakar should suffice to convince people what a crazy idea it is.

As I've said already, I came out of their small apartment on the fourth floor, but seldom by taking the elevator to the first floor and walking through all the archways and yards with their carpet-beating racks, where '50s' carpet-beatings echoed between pastel-colored walls—and perhaps still do. I had much faster routes.

I used to curl up in the window with a view across Riddarfjärden in the winter evenings, reading Heidenstam and Strindberg. The soldiers of Charles XII were there in the winter darkness across the blue-black ice of Riddarfjärden, and Strindberg's Stockholm lay in the darkness on the other side when the fog came, extinguishing the lights on Norr Mälarstrand.

A few years later it was Valéry, Larbaud, and Baudelaire, and I didn't have to move further than the kitchen table to be in Paris of the 1850s. The faint odor of city gas from the stove, which was never quite tight, was enough to give me a touch of an ether high, a slight intoxication that made the shadows in the corners, the towels on their rack, look like hesitant, sad demon faces, or (in the summer) caused the shadows of leaves against the yellow wall to become a room infinitely deep, where whirling galaxies receded further and further from me. I dreamed myself into the lives of the poets, into the yellow circles of the streetlights around a section of sidewalk on autumnal boulevards, the rolling pampas grass in Borges' short stories, abandoned cities in Ecuador, where stepped temples slowly sank into deep verdure.

I didn't see much of Stockholm in my youth, since I spent so much time in a different country, the work of my imagination. In that land I was, unquestionably, what I always should be: poet and ruler at the same time. It was a world that obeyed me, and I didn't really need any other.

It's typical that I don't remember anything from my school years except the endless fantasies while I watched the clock, waiting for the hours to pass. And perhaps the school dances with those wide leather belts and pleated skirts girls wore in those days, the Dixieland music, the smell of sweat, the decorated gym and rather trivial scents.

School was a different world, which I entered and exited according to my own desires.

Exactly the same thing that would one day enable me to live in Casamance without, in fact, being the least bit bothered by matters that usually bother Europeans here, this very thing made me into a poet when I was young.

I had no part in the ordinary world and was not obliged to obey it.

I was going to miss Africa, the red sunsets over the sparse forests of gray baobabs, the small, grass-covered houses in the woods, the apes moving in family groups from treetop to treetop, the city smell of oxidized urine, spices, and chicken droppings, the large red moon on November nights.

But I'd be able to live just as well without Africa as I'd lived without Stockholm as a boy.

Just then I remembered something I hadn't thought about for years: some Saturdays, Papa and I would go first to the Sture Baths and afterward to the movies. There was a kind of voluptuousness that stemmed from the contrast between cold and warm.

5

"Regardless of how you travel," said the governor, "you'll have to go through Dakar, won't you?"

He took his eyes off the ceiling fan for a moment, fastening them on me. In its cold warmth, his gaze reminded me of the picture of a lion in a book entitled *The Wild Beasts of the World* I used to leaf through in the winter evenings of my childhood, after we'd moved to Heleneborgsgatan. The other picture in the book that captured my fancy as strongly represented sperm whales being attacked and torn to pieces by killer whales.

For an instant his gaze confused me to such a degree that I delayed replying, even though I knew that there could be only one answer.

"Of course you might go out through Gambia, but then you'd probably have some complicated formalities to deal with. Frankly, I don't quite understand your objection to going through Dakar."

"Your Excellency, of course I'll go through Dakar."

"That's good. The thing is, you've got some friends. And some of those friends have evidently decided to compensate you for your losses as much as they can."

"Really?"

"I prefer to know nothing about it, and that's a wish I think you can understand. But I have been informed that you will receive a letter in the next few days that will take care of your immediate problems. Where do you want to pick it up?"

"I suggest that my friends, whoever they are and whatever it is that they are able to leave for me, should arrange for me to pick up the envelope at Consul General Erik Koch's in Dakar. He has known me for many years. He's the Swedish consul. May I leave now?"

"For where?"

He looked considerably surprised.

"I have to take a look at the store and see what's happened to my boat. I have no idea what Amadou's been up to these last two weeks."

"I think you've misunderstood me somewhat, my dear Monsieur Bohman. The intention is not for you to walk around Ziguinchor, making new friends and enemies. It is not desirable from my point of view, and you can't be sure that it would be good for you, either. The police officers will conduct you from here directly to a man who will rent you a car."

He rose behind his desk to his full white-clad height, and I took this as a sign that it was time for me to leave.

52

"There are many people who have liked you in Ziguinchor. You leave no large debts and no visible enemies. I wish you good luck."

He lifted the telephone receiver, and the officers of the prefecture were once more in the room. I bowed, and he gave me his hand cordially.

Five minutes later—it can hardly have been more—we were at the local garage, sitting on a bench and waiting for the two garage hands to prepare a well-used jeep for travel.

Thank the Lord, I thought, that they haven't done anything silly with handcuffs or that sort of thing. The officers sat on either side of me, talking merrily.

My only feeling was one of being totally overcome by a sense of homelessness. I must have felt it my whole life, I thought. It's always been as great, but what's happening now is making it visible. These low houses, these large trees, and the river, infinitely broad, with its yellow and gray smells, these white storks in the big trees, these narrow red roads with women carrying children on their heads and men carrying heavy tools—all of it had become a kind of home. Now there's only the river, with its gray smell, disappearing into the fog.

My only homeland is the love I've been able to feel in my life, I thought, as the jeep, a veteran of UNICEF, was provided with oil and questionably new tires.

Anyhow, nobody's any better off.

The river, infinitely broad and gray, under clouds of rising birds, was as impossible to survey as it had always been. And it would always stay the same.

3   The Sea, Always New

1

At the bus stop, among discarded cigarette packages and crumpled tickets, among rusted beer cans and last year's program from the match at Ullevi, coltsfoot was sprouting in large, yellow clumps. Up in the featureless, shabby oak grove on the other side of the street, the hepatica would be out now.

Late as usual for the theater, she was running off at the last minute, worn music case under her arm. Walking the dogs, two large yellow Labradors, took time, and furthermore she didn't have a lot of enthusiasm.

All winter she'd been hoping for Pamina. It was quite clear that they'd do *The Magic Flute* in March, and she knew the visiting English conductor from a brief guest appearance of the whole company at Sadler's Wells in the late '70s. The part was rather an obvious one for her: she'd done it so many times in the '50s. There was something crystalline and abstract about it which had always brought out her best qualities. At the same time as she was teaching a course on the great Modernists at the community music school in Mölndal, she had forced herself to get up early in the morning to go through this score, which she'd had on the music rack since her school days. The penciled notations of at least three different teachers marked the margins like annual rings.

And they had all had different opinions on where to breathe.

Today was Monday, dry and dusty spring weather, with cold puffs from the sea pulling last year's oak leaves into aggressive little whirls, and the bus always late on Mondays. It was supposed to leave at twenty to ten, and it should have been here twelve minutes ago.

Since Friday it had been obvious that she wouldn't get the part. It wasn't easy to say how it had come about. Her rival wasn't particularly beautiful, not particularly young, not particularly glamorous, a singer she'd known since the Opera School and who'd moved around the different theaters as much as she herself had.

It was going to be *The Magic Flute*, but not as many performances as had been expected by any means. Instead they were going to do *The Gypsy Baron*, in which she always used to sing the younger sister. She could sing it in her sleep after ten years in Göteborg.

The theater was under fire. The realities of cultural politics demanded that the Municipal Theater, with its Brecht performances, always enthusiastically received by the critics, and its Swedish Brecht imitations, should get more support. Opera and ballet were high culture. Since opera could only be performed with a bad conscience and operettas proved that the theater did in fact have an audience, it would have to be operettas or, more precisely, the same operettas all the time. Always the same roguish rascals and aristocrats on eternal holiday in Vienna, interminably dancing and drinking champagne.

Most days she (just forty-three and still very beautiful) was able to tell herself that everything could change all of a sudden. She'd get a part that would give her the chance to show what she was capable of. She'd get a big grant from the Academy of Music for studies abroad. Friends from some guest appearance or other would bring up her name when they needed a substitute soprano at the Metropolitan.

She was dressed in a warm, blue cashmere winter coat. Pulled far down on her head she wore a blue cap of the hand-knitted variety, with wool gloves on her small, sensitive hands. She always dressed the most untheatrical, unglamorous way she could think of. She'd never felt at home in the theater. It was a work place, and it had always scared her a little. Her colleagues had an attitude, both toward her and toward their work, which she regarded as vulgar. She came from a different background, from a Stockholm really too old-fashioned to be the childhood milieu of a woman of her generation, a pocket, a protected corner where a way of life much too old had wintered over.

She went faithfully to Stockholm about three times a year even after her father's death in 1962. The apartment was gone. Nowadays she stayed with a woman friend who had an antique store in the Old City. Stockholm in December: the wild swans on Strömmen, the gulls circling the Palace, the wax candles in the December darkness on the green table at the Swedish Academy. (She'd always had a ticket for the Nobel ceremonies through her father, at that time something that was totally taken for granted. Nowadays she had to be content with a few glimpses on TV.)

The building where she had lived with her father (its massive corner balconies embellished with ornamental ironwork) no longer stood on the old corner on Karlavägen. Instead there was a mastodon of a hotel owned by some semipublic forestry corporation.

Not even the people walking on Östermalm nowadays were quite the same. More elegant, perhaps, but totally different, with a different language, a different kind of behavior in shops and at the hairdresser's, a foreign elite that was in the process of taking over the old apartments and who walked their enormous Afghans between the neighborhood bars in the evenings.

The Opera, the Stockholm Opera, was part of the same concept as the candles on the tables at the Academy, the Drottningholm Theater, the summer night concerts at the National Museum in the '50s, when you'd sit on the steps on cushions, listening to Claude Genetay playing chamber music by Brahms and Vivaldi.

Music was something that belonged to large apartments with tall, light windows, with the candles lit against the December darkness. During the great epoch of the Stockholm Opera, in the '50s, when Göran Gentele produced Verdi's *A Masked Ball* and Birgit Nilsson sang the great Wagner parts, then it looked as if music did have a home.

Opera was a landscape you could live in, as naturally as law or medicine, areas her schoolfriends from the Östermalm gymnasiums wanted to inhabit. Music was the true reality. Slush, streetcars where the conductor bickered about lost monthly passes, awful men in cars pursuing you when you got home late from choir practice (so that you had to hold your key ready in your pocket, the exact right key to let yourself in the front door quickly)—all these things were ridiculous distractions, jokes you shared with your classmates when you met for coffee at Tösse's Bakery on Karlavägen.

The real world existed in Händel's oratorios and in the quartets of Mozart's operas. The real world was illusion. And that's what made it real.

After her mother's unexpected death her father remained as brilliant and witty as ever. It almost seemed as if he received new vitality, new energy from his loneliness. His dinners were as famed for their chamber music as for their excellent culinary properties. (As a rule the food came from one of the better caterers and was served by waitresses the family had used for decades. It was always carried in by the kitchen entrance, up a steep staircase with brown wainscoting that she'd been scared of from childhood.)

In his last years he tended to be moody and tired. He'd invite people for lunch and fall asleep over dessert. The one who kept the apartment in some kind of order, always dusting and vacuuming with a striped apron over his short torso, was a former submarine seaman from Sörmland who took the bus all the way from an apartment complex in Hökarängen to take care of his boss, who was almost the same age. This man had used to entertain her classmates with bizarre little anecdotes from the history of the Swedish navy. Above all, of course, the stories were about the first small, steam-driven submarines in the Baltic. There wasn't a captain, not a mate in the submarine service during World War I he didn't remember. He'd also lost at least five buddies when the dying *Ulven* settled in a German minefield one winter's night in 1943.

"Miss Ann-Marie is practicing," he'd used to say, shutting the big sliding doors behind the baby grand. "Miss Ann-Marie is practicing her scales. We won't disturb her."

2

That always made her falter for a little while.

There was fear, lots of fear to live through. And there was the special, sudden fear when a fear stopped. From early on, she had a complicated relationship to her own body. About the time she went through her first period (with an unpleasant feeling that her own body had the capability of becoming nauseating and sticky), she discovered strange new pleasures. There was a lumber room outside the kitchen with cupboards that contained old pails, but also old, shriveled-up tennis shoes from the '20s and a huge yellow can that had once held Baicoli Veneziani. On the front there were silhouettes, in red, of a romantic couple against a deep blue evening sky. Inside the can, which was very hard to open, some objects rolled around. When, to her disappointment, she got it open at last, she found a beautifully painted little armored cruiser made of pewter, no longer than her little finger, a mother-of-pearl pocket knife, a small policeman in the blue uniform of the New York police force, who could walk with oddly short, antlike steps when you wound him up.

Naturally she stole those small objects and hid them under her bed, where Seaman First Class Ahlin never came with his heavy-wheeled vacuum.

She stole with the tickling, pleasurable, and effervescent feeling, not unlike the bubbles in a champagne glass, that girls of a certain age usually experience when they steal: five-kronor bills from Papa's waistcoat (he never kept track of that sort of thing); glass beads from the flower pots in the drawing room; a very small German paperweight with a romantic Rhine landscape on the bottom (it depicted the spot where the river curves to the east by the Lorelei Rock, where twenty years later an American businessman on an intercity train would start something rather like frenetic intercourse with her). Things like that, when you weren't quite sure whether it was real theft to take it or not. Keeping those small objects with her was a way of holding on to the world, perhaps a way of holding on to herself.

The first years after puberty she often had the experience—especially right before her period—that the world was running away from her. Bent over her Latin dictionary, or when she got up too suddenly from stooping over a bookcase, the outside world might—*fall apart*. The light reflections on the intricately patterned Chinese carpet might splinter into what really were, or what might have been had not her own ordering eye been present, spots of intense color arbitrarily arranged in a corner of the endless field of incomprehensible signals which constituted outside reality.

It was difficult to sing during such periods. The voice was there, bell-like and more vigorous than it would ever be in later years; the musical notation was there, with its trills and cadences; the black baby grand willingly lent itself to picking out the melody—but nothing connected. The fragments frightened her.

It was the same way that mechanical toys (the little New York policeman in his blue uniform) frightened her with their mechanical, implacable movements.

Mozart created connections. Even the most daring modulations, the steepest octave leaps, felt necessary. As a seventeen-year-old she'd sung the soprano parts of the *Coronation Mass* one winter night in the Hedvig Eleonora Church, without hesitation, without a trace of nervousness, pure and deep and sincerely united to the melody, to the *connection* in a way she'd perhaps never again experience (in *Svenska Dagbladet*, the next day, the severe Kajsa Rootzén was enchanted). The candles were burning in the church with clear, pure flames. The slight scraping sound as the orchestra settled in for a new passage created a strange effect; it was as if it had said that this music, for one short hour, had moved into the ordinary world.

Singing was difficult or easy, just as there were afternoons when it was impossible to hit the tennis ball and other days when serves and returns sort of stepped by themselves from the center of her own body movements.

A suggestion that was insurmountable for a whole morning became easy if you walked around Humlegården and then quickly settled back at the piano. Actually, difficulty was never the problem: the problem was allowing the music to enter her. When she had a really hard day, it invariably turned out that she'd been thinking of her mother as she sang.

During those years, she often had the feeling of being *observed*, but she didn't quite know by whom. The one *observing* her wanted her to have a certain attitude. Only she didn't know what kind.

Her first communion (prepared for by a private course of study in a rural rectory, when she hurt her calf badly on a bicycle trip: nobody had taught her to bike, and the first time she tried she was expected to do more than twelve miles; the accident happened on a gravelly slope at the end of the run) frightened her. Eating a god had to entail the risk of the god taking root and starting to grow in your stomach.

(In a similar manner, a relative had once warned her against eating watermelon seeds: the melon might take root in her stomach. She actually believed that into her twenties, when a young medical student from the Caroline Hospital, who sometimes took her to the Dramaten Theater, pointed out that the acidic gastric juices don't make a suitable growing ground for melons.)

She didn't have very many friends in school, mostly because visits from her classmates were generally unwelcome and had to be preceded by a couple of day's advance notice to the housekeeper in the kitchen. As a result, and as a result of the fact that in her family school dances were considered rather vulgar, she didn't see many boys outside the classroom the first few years. She did attend some formal dinner parties for young people, with dancing afterward. Although she was already beautiful, she was often left sitting there, mostly chain smoking, after the first duty dance with her dinner partner.

(Later, when she started to sing in earnest, she'd quit smoking for good.)

The boys she met at those dances she had known since they were little. Polite, straight-backed, and well brought up, they talked about what their father said about Erlander, the prime minister, about Lars Forssell and Pär Rådström's cabaret at the Tegnér Restaurant, about Latin exams at the Norra Latin Gymnasium, about the hardships of second-year officer's training at Karlberg.

She didn't understand how a whole tradition weighed on her, how it affected even her way of looking at upholstery fabrics in Svenskt Tenn's shop window. Neither did she understand how strong and also how weak all this made her.

Her first sexual experiences were with men considerably older. She met the first one on a ship to England the summer of '52, when she was going to a language course in Sussex.

He followed her from a dance in the ship's bar to her cabin, and she lost her virginity with such ease that she was never able to pinpoint the moment when it happened. The experience was incredibly intense, and afterward she never really wanted to admit it to herself. She connected this sudden and extremely experienced lover with the slightly repulsive phenomenon of the little white hairs on his wrists. In her dreams, she was often pursued by the feeling that someone had tried to penetrate her childhood and take possession of it.

Even in Sussex, she was harassed for some time by telephone calls from this man, who evidently stayed in England all summer. There was just one telephone for the students, in the anteroom to the headmaster's office, which smelled of dust and mint and where the secretaries sat. These conversations, which she always tried to keep as brief and discouraging as possible, embarrassed her greatly. Still, they were to meet again.

The whole episode made her feel panic-stricken, and it delayed her first great love—she always spoke about such experiences rather in the language of women's journals, using words she'd never have dreamed of using about music—by three or four years, she no longer remembered exactly.

3

When the bus came at last it was packed, in spite of the fact that the start of the route was only a few blocks back. Young people in down jackets, with ice hockey implements in big canvas bags wedged between the seats, pale retirees going into town to get food bargains at the farmers' market (forgetting the price of the bus ticket), three obligatory morning drunks who tried, without much success, to inspire the passengers in front of the bus to a sing-along.

Young women with hard faces usually dominated the bus at this time of day. Perhaps they worked in banks or offices.

She tried to imagine their lives, their nights, their dreams, and their hopes, but she could read nothing but disappointment in their faces.

The enforced contact with other people, in buses, in depart-ment stores, at the post office, in the opera company as well, actually made her much more tired than any kind of work could.

The lives of others seemed more and more difficult to understand the older she got. She had just one thought concerning the hard faces on the bus: it looked as if they'd never had an impulse to do good, but not to do evil, either. They'd simply never had the chance to make any real decisions.

Almost simultaneously, just as the mechanical strain of going around a traffic circle seemed about to press a large man's equally large suitcase into her diaphragm, she asked herself: Have I ever had that chance?

In some ways she had. Not once but many times. And every single time, with similar ease, she'd managed to avoid everything essential in her life.

It had made things a lot easier. But always there was this feeling of living on the border line of the barely endurable. From Göta Place it was just a short walk to the theater. Still, the gusts had such force that they constantly seemed about to tear the worn music case out of her hands. The first spring storm was on its way. On the other side of the canal, where a crumpled newspaper drifted back and forth like a demented swan hunting its lost Lohengrin as the squalls echoed between the stone facings, the street was blocked off because a metal roof was coming down the front of one of the older houses.

It looks quite ridiculous, she thought, as if the house for some reason could no longer stand to show its face.

Once through the doors of the stage entrance, which had an uncanny ability to close behind you with a frightful bang, she realized that she was at least twenty minutes late for the rehearsal pianist, a mild, disillusioned Polish refugee from the spring of '68. She found him by the grand piano, immersed in one of his ever-lasting Polish exile journals. He greeted her with an absent-minded smile and kissed her hand with the same mechanical precision he'd used for the last three years.

"Forgive me, Zbigniew, but there's a storm out there. The buses were running late."

"Oh, it doesn't matter, I've had such an interesting time with a man who explained the ideological grounds of Solidarity."

"Has anyone else been looking for me?"

65

"The boss was here a while ago. He wanted you to look in for a minute before the afternoon rehearsal. But it wasn't anything important, he said."

"Has Ulla been in?"

"What do you mean, in?"

"I mean, has Ulla been with you today?"

"Yes, between nine and ten."

"Is she over her cold?"

"She's back in form."

"She seemed so down the other day."

"I didn't notice. Perhaps that was just when she was speaking to you. Where do you want to start today?"

"I have a marker at bar 270. But I'd like to start over with those lousy lines just before . . . Zbigniew, do you think that what we're doing here is meaningful? Are we creating art?"

Zbigniew, never particularly talkative, preferred playing to answering. Not the beginning of the second act of the *Gypsy Baron*, however, but the hectic, at once passionate and cold chords that introduce the aria of the Queen of Night. And Ann-Marie sang, but in a voice that wasn't warmed up at all, that was perhaps a bit strained, right up to the hellish octave leaps in the coloratura part. Her rhythm and breathing lost, she sank down on the nearest chair with her arms across the back. From behind it looked as if she were crying.

At that moment she was all alone, floating in the namelessness which exists between art and the darkness where art is not. A cold rain lashed the large, hospital-like windows of the rehearsal hall.

I have left a world, she thought, the ordinary world, where there are people, children, silence over the breakfast cereal, quiet conversations over the evening papers, summer cottages and fishing trips, a world where you have a family, go to the movies on Friday afternoons and where someone is nice enough to help you rinse the dinner dishes. An ordinary, vulgar world, where nothing means anything in particular.

All just because I searched for a different world which I once glimpsed as a child: the pure, complete world of art, of perfection. Not from a desire for fame but because I believed that's where I belonged.

I knew that I belonged there. But that world didn't welcome me. I wasn't the right kind. Now I have nowhere to live, nowhere at all.

Several minutes must have passed. Zbigniew put his arm across her shoulders. He couldn't help noticing how strong they were.

"Don't you want to take your coat off?"

"No," she said. "I think I'll sing with my coat on for a while. I'm cold."

4

In the 1950s, the Hovedbanegaard, Copenhagen's main train station, had something indescribably festive about it, at least for young Swedes who changed trains there on their way to countries beyond that felt freshly opened, adventurous to visit. The white steam from the continental trains rose under wrought-iron arches; people dragging oversized backpacks up and down the steep flights of stairs; the three different restaurants with their surprising, deep-green beer bottles and generous drinks of aquavit; the incredibly fat open-faced sandwiches; the teasing incomprehensibility of a language that always made you think you had understood what was being said while you really hadn't; the strange counting words, as complicated as a moon calendar from ancient Assyria; the City Hall bells and the odd, close-packed throngs of cyclists who braved a never-ending flow of traffic: everything conveyed the impression of a more festive, more exhilarating world than that of still newly awakened Sweden on the other side of the Sound, a country which had just taken off its winter furs.

It was on one of the platforms, where the loudspeaker even talked German and English and called out exotic destinations like Belgrade, Paris, and Munich, that she was going to say good-bye to Hasse. The idea was that twenty minutes later, she would take the train in the opposite direction, to Malmö, and meet Jan in time to see Ingmar Bergman's new and remarkable production of *Faust* at the State Theater. They'd spent the night at the Mission Hotel on Vesterbrogade and, for a change, they'd mostly talked. In spite of its name the hotel was rather shabby and noisy, and they'd had no trouble checking in. It sounded as if whole teams of handball players were rushing in and out of their rooms, changing and showering for a new half, all night long.

It was quite impossible to remember what they had talked about, just that it was a very intense conversation, intense as conversation could only be at that time. It must have been about their separation, about not seeing each other any more.

She could still remember a brown lampshade made from parchment, or from some kind of dry, dusty-smelling paper that pretended to be parchment, and that the brown lampshade slid down all the time so that the cold light of the naked bulb fell on them. It was the only time she'd ever seen him cry.

Now, around eleven o'clock, after they'd had breakfast at the Hovedbanegaard and shared a bottle of Carlsberg, they felt unaccountably merry. Everything, the night, the journey, the tears, the future, suddenly looked like a bad joke. Flocks of gulls fluttered over the City Hall Square, and the world was large and open.

"I'll come with you to Malmö."

"But I'm supposed to meet Jan there."

"Where's your seat? In the orchestra?"

"Are you sure we'll go to the theater?"

"No. We don't have to go there."

Strangely enough it didn't occur to them, not for a single moment, that if she wasn't going to meet Jan at the theater (he had been sent down by some paper in Stockholm to write "poetically" of the event and had called her hopefully since the middle of August) there wasn't much point in going to Malmö. They might just as well have gone to Hälsingborg, or to Falsterbo for that matter.

They went to Malmö, possibly because that's where the train went. After crossing the Sound in rather choppy weather—the beautiful, clear fall days were apparently turning into a gray, hostile, real fall—they found themselves at the Central Station.

"Now what do we do?" Ann-Marie said.

"I don't know," Hasse said.

Their enthusiasm, the feeling that it was a good joke, had somehow fallen from them in the course of the trip. The wind was tearing at the yellow leaves which dropped into the canal one by one; they skated back and forth on the surface as aggressive little gusts took hold of them.

"We might go to the City Theater and see whether they have any tickets left," Hasse said.

"We'll run into Jan."

"Sooner or later, you'll have to talk to him anyway."

There were tickets. The weather had done its share.

The lobby was surprisingly elegant, full of people. They didn't see Jan.

The women at the well buzzed. Max von Sydow, magnificent with his long, narrow head, explained:

> "With fervent zeal I have pursued
> deep studies in philosophy;
> law and medicine ensued;
> concluding with theology,
> here I stand, no wit the wiser"

—something that made Ann-Marie think of Uppsala, a city she didn't want to think about right then. Mephistopheles, played by Toiwo Pawlo, was suddenly there on stage, without having made an entrance, small, with quicksilver movements. He pronounces each line as a lesson he has learned by heart, because he has heard and said the same things so many times before, since the beginning of mankind. He's tired, and in his tiredness there is tremendous force: a downhill slope.

She had seen Jan long before Act One was over, before she knew that she had seen him, in fact. As expected, he was sitting far in front with an empty seat beside him, his chin in his hand in a way that she recognized.

Oh, that's where she had heard those tired cadences before!

There was a strange resemblance between Mephistopheles on stage and that prematurely round-shouldered poet with his garret in Uppsala. He is no Faust, he is Mephistopheles, and just by sitting there with an empty seat next to him, he forces me to him whether I want it or not. A straight, clean, clear person like Hasse will never understand it, and I'd better never explain it to him.

Mephistopheles has been sitting there all the time, smiling slightly, luring us on. That's how it is. And now it's fall in the park below, and as early as the first act, everything is hopeless.

In the intermission she said to Hasse, "It's hopeless. I've known all the time that it's hopeless."

"You mean you have to speak to him?"

"I'm afraid so."

He looked at her long and attentively, as if he were seeing her for the first time. She had the feeling that she was the object of *scientific* scrutiny, as a chemist investigating what strange matter might be interfering with his spectrogram, giving it unexpected lines at a wavelength where they ought not to be.

Perhaps, she thought, quite calmly, perhaps he has to be like that. He always thinks he has to kill something in himself in order to show his strength. It would probably be better if he allowed himself to break, sometime.

But she couldn't possibly imagine how that might happen. Breaking was simply not his specialty.

"I'm leaving now," he said. "I'll give you the ticket for the coat room. I've already got the number."

"Bye then. Take care of yourself."

"You're the one who's supposed to take care. But don't try to find me again. Don't write. Don't call. I'll never again be able to trust you. I'll try something else now."

She had a silly feeling that she had absolutely nothing to say. Not only that. Everything was already a stage, a piece of bad theater, framed by a piece of good theater. She simply was no longer able to think of anything interesting enough to say. She waved at him and went with large, very dark blue, very preoccupied eyes into the theater. At such times, she had a hesitant, somewhat dragging step, reminiscent of a polar bear in a zoo.

70

My God, she thought, what a bizarre story. I don't want many more bizarre stories like that in my life.

The buzz in the theater had already stopped.

5

There had been a number of different managers at the theater the last fifteen years. This one was still quite new. He'd been the first to introduce a kind of contraption with ENGAGED—WAIT—COME IN by his door. It would have been unthinkable in the '50s. She didn't know much more about him than that his name was Niklas Wedelin and that he always wanted people to call him Nicke when he led personnel rap sessions. After the "last battle," as the actors referred to the latest complicated two-front war with the Municipal Theater, local government delegates, and their own theater, too devoted to "high culture," Nicke had been called in from Norrköping to deal with their problems. He was the new type of manager produced by grotesque democratic business practices: a soft, elusive boy with long brown hair and outsize glasses. The teddy bear type of boss, a specialist in getting people to agree to orderly little compromises.

She'd liked her former boss a whole lot better. Sigge Thelander was the product of '60s Stockholm; he came from a background which still indulged in Social-Democratic cultural jamborees at the Modern Museum, the merry, state-subsidized society of culture pundits Harry Schein and Pontus Hulten. It was the period when people went to New York to see how things should be done.

The country was small. It had always imported most of its ideas. Once, in a distant grandfather era, it was Paris and Berlin that Stockholm sought to emulate. In the '60s it was New York. The galleries on 57th Street, the Museum of Modern Art, and the happenings in the Garden there and at the Armory would be transposed to museums and theaters in Stockholm. It never quite came off, since a large part of the audience didn't understand that you were actually supposed to be in New York.

Sigge eventually ended up in Göteborg with the express charge of getting high culture at the Music Theater under control. The first season he sandwiched a gigantic happening with concrete poetry and huge screens between a performance of *The Barber of Seville* and another of *The White Horse Inn*. The result was somewhat uneven, but the papers, in particular the Stockholm ones, praised it to the skies.

Sigge had a peculiarity. He hated opera. This didn't mean that he worked against opera, just that he wanted to "expose" it. Opera was one of the best ways to expose myths about art. Behind the euphony there was nothing but low concerns: sensuality, lechery. There were no geniuses, only upstarts who displayed themselves in front of audiences. Sigge was the son of an elementary school teacher in Norrland and a Methodist clergyman who'd died young. He'd been brought up in a milieu totally devoid of art, of beauty, of euphony: the kind of home where people turn off the radio when it starts to play Mozart.

Out of this, he constructed a democratic esthetic program.

Sarastro had to be played as a disgusting old pimp from Malmskillnadsgatan. The Duke in *Rigoletto* had to fart between arias. The Three Genii in *The Magic Flute* had to make their entrance in bib overalls with wrenches in their back pockets. The underlying principle of this esthetic was that everything was something else at bottom. Art was a mixture of lechery, envy, and lust for power, and it had to be brought back to its origins.

In the words of an Italian guest conductor, Vario Varossi from Milan, who was at the theater for a couple of months and then broke his contract prematurely: "He has created an artistic program from the fact that he knows nothing about art. Since he can't forbid it, he has to ignore it."

Paradoxically, many people found it rather fun. Ann-Marie had always had a liking for farce and parody. She thought it was entertaining when the dragon in *Siegfried* turned up in a diving suit and sang "Was stört mich?" without opening the glass front on his helmet. Furthermore, the theater received flattering publicity for the first time in many years. People came from as far away as Copenhagen to see what was happening.

"There is always," Varossi used to say, "secret pleasure in seeing things and personalities dethroned."

He himself returned to Milan to forge perfect Verdi performances with the deep-red copper sheen that was the glory of the ancestors.

Sigge might have continued indefinitely, taking the curtains down from the windows, so to speak, exhibiting the manifold sins and wickedness of Wagner, Monteverdi, and Mozart, if only there had been enough geniuses. By and by, there was hardly anyone left to dethrone. New York wasn't quite the same either, and Sigge had stopped going there a long time ago, as he got somewhat lazy with increasing age and started to prefer warmer climes.

It wasn't his view of opera that became his downfall but a battle with the personnel committee at the theater. It didn't have to do with parts or conductors but with keys.

For decades, some of the senior colleagues had had their own keys to the stage entrance: the conductors who had to get ready for rehearsals, certain singers who considered they needed keys. Some time in the early '70s, scores, old cast photos in the lobby, even musical instruments, started disappearing from the theater. Police investigation led nowhere. It was obvious that someone who had keys was stealing like a magpie. Sigge sent out a memo in which he simply called in all keys. He was a child of the innocent '60s, when newspaper editors were still appointed in board rooms and not by employee vote, when directors were able to decide which plays should be performed without a ballot by the whole work force.

Poor Sigge didn't understand what a hornet's nest he'd stirred up. In the course of a few successful years, he'd fallen in love with his theater. He didn't like photos from the '30s and flutes costing ten thousand kronor disappearing every other night. Consequently he persisted: the keys had to be collected. Unfortunately he'd forgotten that this was the year his contract was up for renewal. It now transpired that a united Employees' Association had another candidate on its slate, namely the economist, music lover, and amateur actor Anders Niklas Wedelin. After getting his degree in business, he'd started his career by settling complicated employee problems in a chain of department stores around Norrköping, then had a brief spell as an administrator at the National Board of Culture. It was general knowledge that he was a Social Democrat and interested in music, and the tip had actually come from a government agency, National Concerts.

He arrived at New Year's, started by asking everyone to call him Nicke and telling them how terribly inexperienced he was, and that they'd all have to help him and be a proper team if the theater were ever to amount to anything. Times were bad and appropriations for cultural activities were threatened by dark forces on the right, who in recent years had appropriated cabinet posts and were now engaged in extensive cultural cutbacks. In short, if the theater were to survive, they'd have to make strenuous efforts. The first thing he wanted to do was introduce a whole new subscription system which would distribute tickets in the work place and in clubs.

As far as the keys were concerned, they were never returned. In some fabulous manner, Nicke always prevented the question from cropping up on the agenda.

She had no idea what he wanted this time. Suddenly the door signal changed to green. Nicke, surrounded by dubious artworks from the more feeble local galleries, at his desk of antique oak, facing a filing cabinet of galvanized metal, received her.

"Hi, Ann-Marie, how *are* you?"

"Just fine, thanks."

"Your new part feels good?"

"It doesn't feel like anything. I've done it so many times."

"I heard you had a problem with Karin doing Pamina."

"What do you mean, a problem? It was unfair."

"That's how it felt to you?"

"Listen, Nicke, and try to understand what I'm saying: you use a jargon that transforms everything into expressions of emotion. People have a problem with something, something feels right or wrong. That way, you manage to turn everyone else's judgments or wishes into something subjective. Your own wishes are the only things that have any kind of objectivity around here, the only things that retain the character of facts."

"Sit down, Ann-Marie, grab a chair. Let's see if we can't come up with something that'll feel right to you."

She realized that she had an arduous half-hour in front of her. Either he'd suggest that she go on leave for a while to teach evening courses, or else the time had come around again for the old idea about performances and concerts in public libraries. That would keep her busy until late spring.

Suddenly it was clear to her that what she was experiencing now was exactly the phenomenon that once, as late as the '50s, was referred to as getting "dismissed." They're firing me, she thought. They're firing me, plain and simple, after twenty years at the theater, twenty years in which I never really had a chance to accomplish what I wanted to do here. It was never within my reach. Basically, it's my own fault. They're firing me because I've never had a profile here. They've never been able to experience me as a presence. I didn't belong. She surfaced from her thoughts long enough to hear Nicke grinding away on his own:

"What I believe, don't you see, it that people in the environs here will never discover the theater unless the theater comes to them."

"So you're thinking of asking the city to establish a kind of consulting position. Then this consulting person is to travel around, telling children and retirees at the public libraries about nice old Mozart and nice old Beethoven."

"*How* could you guess what I was going to say? Has someone told you?"

"No. You see, I wasn't listening all that closely. So I didn't know just where you had gotten to. The next step is for you to offer me the consultant job."

"Have you been talking to Roffe?"

Roffe chaired the Artists' Association. If she had been discussed with him the thing was probably already settled.

"No. But I realize that you want to offer me that job. My time as a singer is over, in other words?"

"That kind of consulting job is almost three times the money. Not to mention how much better your hours will be."

"That's very nice of you. I think there are many people who would be happy to have such an opportunity. Really very nice of you to think of me."

The view through the window captured her attention. It seemed there were more roofs in danger of blowing off in the storm; men carrying sawhorses and blinking warning lights were blocking off the street beyond. How often had she hurried across that street after a performance, freshly showered and changed, in her usual blue cashmere coat, and still with that whole other world, music, present in her heartbeats?

"I wouldn't get into this whole thing except that I know there *may* be cutbacks later on. My budget is strictly emergency rations."

"Of course," she said, continuing to look out the window. "Of course. I'm very sorry I have to be in your budget. I shouldn't be in anyone's budget."

He flapped his hands in a sudden childish gesture. In all his experience, there had been nothing like her. Slowly, a feeling of reluctant admiration took possession of him. There are, he thought, people who are like stones. They're no good to anyone. They don't fit in anywhere. Exactly because they're no use they acquire a kind of authority which none of us useful people will ever have.

Meanwhile, her thoughts were with the flock of seagulls the storm was flinging wildly from one compass point to another. Ever since she was little, she'd always had a hard time keeping her attention on things that didn't interest her.

Her present life was one of those things.

4   A Rent in the Web of Time

1

The 747 was climbing steadily over Cape Cod into cloudless skies; a crystalline winter sun broke in through the windows like a revelation, and the large plane settled onto an easterly course which would bring it to the northern tip of Ireland in five hours and then toward other destinations. The "No Smoking" signs were turned off, and he could hear the promising sound of stewardesses rattling ice cubes in whiskey glasses. He himself had stopped smoking, but he drank quite a few whiskeys instead.

He was back in the sea of air.

The night before he had done his laundry as usual in the laundromat by the Star Supermarket. While the machines worked and washed two weeks of laundry, they, his wife Priscilla and he, had gone as usual to O'Henry's Bar at the corner of Beacon and Sacramento.

They'd always have a beer there while the laundry sloshed around in the machine. It was a spot where you could have the most thoroughgoing family fights without disturbing anyone for a second, since there were two TVs, each tuned to its own channel, replete with gunfire, car chases, airplane crashes, and exploding buildings. As if that weren't enough, a huge jukebox filled the already vibrating room with hard rock. Now and then a dynamite blast from the construction work in the subway under them made the whole building shake. The construction crew in their red hardhats would often sit at the bar, playing cards. When he fought with Priscilla there was nothing tragic or distressing about it. It was a loving occupation, a game, a form of contact. Her long, red, Irish hair tossed back and forth; her green eyes made her look like a Pre-Raphaelite witch. He'd always had a soft spot for witches. If you had a tendency toward the Romantic usage of former times, you might say they were his destiny.

The next morning, of course, it was quite impossible to remember what they'd fought about that particular night. They could fight about anything, from TV channels to women's groups' demonstrations. The only thing they consistently refused to fight about were sex and money. She had a slim, tall, flat figure, with negligible breasts. Her skirts, often made of leather, clung to her thighs in an almost boyish manner.

She was the kind of woman you often saw on the Harvard campus. The standard type, so to speak.

They were much better than they looked, but they easily turned into witches.

He leaned back with a sigh in his first-class seat and unfolded the morning edition of *The Boston Globe*. Just the usual peace demonstrations in Germany.

Yes, they're marching again, he thought.

He was a complete, hardened cynic.

He was on his way to the head office of the International Atomic Energy Commission in Vienna to present a report from his own little consulting firm. Three days a week he lectured at the Harvard Science Center and saw his graduate students in the afternoon to discuss their experiments and reports. The rest of the week he worked on his own projects.

He'd long ago gotten used to this kind of life. Not only gotten used to, he loved it. His children no longer disturbed him. The older girl was at a progressive boarding school for gifted children in upstate New York, where she was doing something that, at least from a distance, looked suspiciously like Creative Writing, and the younger one was so interested in horses that they never saw her before bedtime.

Only the witch and he were home, and they were happy every time they saw each other.

The clouds were now far below them; they wandered back toward the horizon in a slow row. Like sheep. Home to Boston.

He punched the secret combination to the lock on his briefcase, got out a fistful of papers, and started reading.

He was seldom prepared when he boarded a plane. But he usually was when he got off.

Beginning of March 1981: Tentative project submitted to the Ministerial Council.

February 1982: Ministerial Council distributes the text to the governments of member nations and international organizations for consultation.

November 1982: (deadline) Member governments and international organizations report on the results of the consultations in which they have participated.

March 1983: (five days in Vienna) Group meeting. Preparations for final project.

April 1983: Final project submitted to all delegations of Ministerial Council.

June 1983: Ministerial Council establishes final text for transmission to member governments . . .

He moved stiffly in his seat, tossing his heavy body impatiently from side to side as he read. The mixture of heaviness and impatience was his strength. People who didn't know him well were often surprised at how quickly he could get up to the net when required, just as they were surprised that his let balls, as distinct from those of nearly every other amateur player, went over the net almost without exception. He tended to come across as someone without imagination, highly objective, professional, dressed in the kind of chalk-striped suit that was the uniform of professionals in his world. Only a few friends, for instance at the Harvard Faculty Club, knew that he could sometimes be tempted to recite poetry in the lounge, when the conversation got around to bizarre world events, or to the most bizarre secrets of some particular colleague. He made no secret of the fact that once upon a time he'd been drawn to imagination, to fantasy, and that he had consorted with some of the most esoteric poets in Stockholm in the '50s. If a Swedish poet, Tranströmer for example, came to do a reading in the Farnsworth Room, he'd be there, a silent, somewhat melancholy professorial type among the group of literary ladies and Scandinavian students, never asking any questions in the official discussion period but curious afterward over a glass of wine. Forssell was in the Academy now, was he? How about Staffan Larsson? Had he published any new books of poems? It seemed the answers he got were never quite what he'd expected.

As the years passed, he came to see Europe more and more as a collection of conference hotels where the same somber men in identical suits discussed the control of fissionable matter and new inspection conditions for reactor plants. These conference rooms, with their bottles of mineral water and stacks of xeroxes, were in a way extensions of his own office, of the warm innards of a tall office building in cold, wintry Boston, where you'd see the snow whirling around Quincy Hall at Christmas time. The Europe he once left was a different Europe from the one he visited professionally four or five times a year. Perhaps it occupied a different time-line in a science fiction novel.

Not even his detractors denied he had a certain grim sense of humor. It was most obvious where his profession was concerned. The last ten years, he had spent most of his time on the not unprofitable task of giving advice to those who, for various and different reasons, wanted to prevent the proliferation of fissionable matter in the world. He seldom expressed any private opinion, despised journalists who had opinions on the matter, and detested snap judgments on almost anything. At the same time, it was hardly a secret that he considered the whole thing impracticable, or anyway extremely difficult to put into practice. There was a fundamental contradiction in everything he did. It made him more and more successful, more and more wealthy and important, and his task resembled an addition of negative fractions which got closer and closer to zero.

He lived in a world, the United States of the early '80s, that dreamed of a new innocence, new beginnings, a return to old virtues, a green world that would rise from the sea. But was there any room in the real world for that kind of hope? Perhaps the world had lost the last of its innocence, once and for all, when nuclear weapons had found their way, in August of 1945, out of the terrible Pandora's box that was history? Trying to shut the doors again felt like closing the gate of a lock manually against the full pressure of the water in the lock basin.

He'd never really understood what the others wanted. Why weren't they able to act rationally? Almost everyone he'd met had somehow seemed distanced from the consequences of their own actions. They didn't see where they were going.

For short periods of Manichean brooding he might succumb

to the thought that perhaps the purpose of humans was not that they should be rational, and that disorder, peril, chaos, suspended like a two-edged sword over the festive board, was the natural condition of the game.

Anyway, he'd known a couple of people who lived just that way. Perhaps that was a happier way to be.

One of those he thought of right away was Jan. Jan with his shy, apologetic smile. There was some sort of black hole in him that was nourished by his own existence but which, at the same time, made him invulnerable.

The only ones who'd survive in the long run were those who lived as if survival were unimportant.

2

He wanted to *catch hold.* Without knowing precisely what he was looking for, he was almost always examining his memory for something, perhaps a crack in his life. It would, he thought, explain something about his own feeling of not quite *belonging.*

There were episodes of a peculiarly rich color, of heavy existence, which performed in a strange way in the context of his life, as if they'd had a life of their own.

He remembered a thunderstorm over his father's summer house in northern Västmanland in the summer of '52, when the thunder turned into a shower of hailstones weighing several hundred grams that threw up thick jets from the lake, damaged all the car roofs, and broke the windows in all the greenhouses in the whole district. Sixteen years old, he'd stood by the window watching the storm come and go, feeling a blind excitement. There were moments like that, when life promised other powers, different constellations than what it ought to contain according to normal covenants.

Thinking of those things was no good. It introduced a mixture of anxiety and sadness which made the world look like a continuous, smooth body of water.

But the descent of this atmosphere, gray, dull as lead, over his world was sometimes a sign that the strong, the life-giving forces were approaching.

The scientific ideas which had made him one of Sweden's youngest professors of applied physics in the early '60s had been of that kind. There was a state of *grace* when everything could be thought, where all ordinary obstacles were swept away and everything, all of a sudden, allowed itself to be combined with everything else.

Long, warm summer days in the '50s (in particular, he remembered the summer of '55; it was so hot and dry that it became legendary) he used to sit down by the lakeshore, where brown water flowed over round rocks, and look at the schools of minnows coming into the shallowest water.

If you threw a small rock at the middle of the school, it scattered with lightning speed, in fact as soon as the shadow of the rock fell across the water. If you threw the rock at the edge of the school instead, you could see that the fish scattered with equal speed on the right and left sides of the school. They all scattered at the same time, as if the school were an electromagnetic field.

As a boy, he was a pagan in the sense that he conceived of nature as a part of himself and himself as a part of nature. It had made him into a physicist and left something unresolved behind.

In 1979 he'd been to a St. Lucia day celebration at the Swedish Club in Boston. He was just sitting there with his red-haired daughter (who had just been given a saddle horse and only lived for things to do with the stable) when a small, bald man came up to him. He seemed strangely tense, almost trembling, and approached him with such determination (like a torpedo boat in open water) that for one second he wondered if it was an *assault* of some kind.

"Good Lord, how scared I used to be of you, Hasse."

(Only people who didn't know him but wanted to pretend they did called him "Hasse" instead of Hans nowadays.)

"Excuse me, but have we met before?" (From close up, the man had something that reminded him of something. The unusually large, almost pointed ears, the tilted eyebrows, gave him a feeling of having seen the man before, not in real life but in a fairy-tale illustration, a benevolent gnome or gremlin under some fir tree or other in the woods. Did it have to be a *benevolent* gnome, by the way?)

"How do you suppose I'd be scared of you if we've never met?" By now he is searching his memory frantically for ill-treated Ph.D. candidates, for people whose articles he'd criticized in professional journals, for people he'd refused to recommend for jobs and fellowships; he's about to run every tennis player he's ever met through his memory, when the gnome continues: "Of course you don't remember that you were quite fond of throwing rocks in those days?"

"Yes, into the water, to see the minnows scatter."

"Not just at minnows."

"What the hell do you mean . . . what's your name, anyway?"

"Per Olof."

"Per Olof?"

"Granberger."

"Your father had a summer cottage further down the road?"

(A vague memory surfaces, not of a small boy but of an incensed older man with a walking stick who'd pass at great speed on his afternoon walk, checking his pace with a stop watch.)

"That's right. And every day he'd send me to fetch the mail at the mailboxes, on a lady's bike that was much too big for me."

"But that must have been fun?"

"No. It wasn't fun at all. Imagine a skinny, insecure thirteen-year-old on a lady's bike that's much too big for him, his hands full of letters and newspapers and packages . . . ."

"Yes, that can be difficult."

"And then there's a horrible little seven-year-old behind the fence, throwing rocks."

"Throwing rocks?"

"Yes. With uncanny precision. One on the temple, one right on the hand that's holding the mail. Then you'd laugh, just roar with laughter, when I took a spill with everything."

"Are you sure it was me?"

"Of course it was you. There were only two kids that age then."

"I always thought it was the minnows I threw rocks at."

After another couple of glasses of the club's very strong but also quite eccentric wine punch, they had reconciled. He'd promised never again to throw rocks at Per Olof Granberger, architect.

"Architect, a fine profession. Great to have an occupation that combines artistic vision and advanced technology, isn't it?"

"I'm an architect with the Fortifications Administration. That's the reason I'm here for a conference."

"What do you build?"

"Defenses."

The purser, a younger man with very little space between his eyes, humorous, friendly eyes, who was now leaning forward to ask if he wanted anything else before dinner, reminded him, no, not of Jan, he'd met Jan at the same time as he'd finally managed to cut loose from a girl, Ann-Marie, but of a friend from school who somehow was Jan's prototype.

(There are, in everyone's life, long chains of people who somehow are each other's prototypes, or perhaps you could call them precursors.)

At that time, there was a species of black pond mussels in the Kolbäck River, up by Seglingsberg's Locks, but never any farther north. They were totally inedible but fun to dive for and pick out of the mud. That boy, whose name was Mac, had an uncanny knack for finding them. His father must have been a Scot: there was something vaguely foreign about him. In the kitchen of the summer cottage there were the most fantastic old cans with English biscuit brand names and insignia on them, containing screws, nails, old spools of thread, fishing line, hooks. His mother, small, kind, and absent-minded, hardly ever had anything to say when he came to ask if Mac could come out with him to the raft. There was a kind of tired, absent-minded, resigned but humorous atmosphere in the family that he wasn't used to from his own home and which often confused him. They seemed to have no ambition.

The world was the way it was, and they were satisfied with it, or at least they didn't expect anything new from it.

Lying on the raft, drifting in the afternoon heat as a solitary seagull moved with anxious cries across the endless delta country (it felt endless then), enclosed in the strange green smell of the bulrushes, they'd often do what they called "parodies." They parodied their teachers, the voices on the radio news (at that time, they always talked about the Korean War); they parodied the great poets of the day, Lindegren, Vennberg. They became absorbed, choked with laughter in verbal games like:

Able I was ere I saw Elba.
Candy is dandy, but liquor is quicker.

and one that might have come from Mac's father:

Vice is nice, incest is best.

They approached those games in ways that were a little different. No, quite a bit different. For Hans there was a kind of fundamental joy that the world could become complicated, that symbols could be turned inside out. For Mac it was much more serious: a way of distancing himself from the whole world. There was not a text, not a newspaper headline, not a recipe that he couldn't turn into something ridiculous.

It was as if he wanted to turn the very attempt to describe the world into a joke. A weak sunset breeze drove the raft through channels in the rushes. Sometimes they might encounter a pair of cranes that disappeared into open water with nasal, trumpeting sounds.

"Flying trumpets," Mac said. The sunset breeze set the raft moving again. Summer held them and would keep them for a long time. Their friendship was too brittle ever to be mentioned.

He had no recollection of where Mac disappeared to. The last time he'd heard from him was when he was around nineteen, when he did his military service in the navy and served in mid-

winter up in the Gulf of Bothnia on the icebreaker *Ymer*. The
letter Mac wrote was rather dry and humorless.

In his dreams, he often confused Mac and Jan. They had
something in common.

3

One sunny, ice-cold, clear winter day when he drove from central
Boston along the Charles to Harvard and was just waiting for the
traffic light to turn green at the Larz Anderson Bridge, an eight-
man shell passed under the bridge. It was pretty to watch.

The measured movements of the rowers, the light foam
around the narrow, mahogany-gleaming prow, the drops of
water falling from the oar blades curved like the feet of a rising
waterbird. The coach, in a green motorboat fifty yards back in
their wash, was shouting instructions, inaudible to him in the
heavy morning traffic across the bridge.

That moment a memory struck him, similar to the way a
meteor which has been on its way for a long time in the empty,
meaningless darkness outside the Solar System will at last be
captured by the Earth's attraction and land there. It was a
memory that hadn't made itself heard for a single second in
twenty years and which was suddenly there, crystalline, impera-
tive:

I've left ten bottles of cider in a cellar in Oxford.
For twenty-three years, they've been waiting in a cellar.

April 1957. A thin rain across Broad Street, a flow of students
on their bikes, all in their black gowns, just an occasional car:
they look like a flock of crows. Shoes muddy from his having
walked across Christ Church Meadow, purely out of absent-
mindedness, although he knows that the lane is almost impassable, he arrives, twenty minutes late, at the pub above the Exam-
ination Schools and almost gets tangled up in the rows of um-
brellas spread out to dry on the heavy, beer-smelling coco
matting by the door. In the weak illumination, in the smell of
damp wool, and obsessed with the thought that *he can't stand it
another day*, he goes up to the counter where the kindly Danish

philosopher Kasterud is waiting, wearing over his shoulders the kind of duffel coat made from yellow, felt-like wool which was so popular then. There was always something priestly about him, with a pale, narrow face that always, somehow, made you think of the characters in the Danish filmmaker Carl Dreyer's great movies. This priestly trait expressed itself, at that time, in the fact that Kasterud listened, faithfully and mildly, and without giving a lot of advice, to other people's problems. Some twenty years later, he became a bishop in the Danish church, something Hans would never know, since Danish diocesan publications are not read very frequently at Harvard or in Boston clubs.

"How goes it? Did you go to Austin's lecture?"

"No. I didn't go. I walked around Christ Church Meadow a while instead."

"In this weather?"

"Ye-es."

"You're having a bad time?"

"*I can't stand it another day.*"

"Why don't you move out on her? Are you that much in love with her?"

"I'm not that much in love with her any longer. It's something else that scares me."

"What?"

"I think she's going mad."

"How do you know when someone's going mad?"

"I know."

As someone doing research, he had the right to live outside the college walls. He had appreciated it. The breakfast conversation in the dark, oak-laden dining room of Magdalen College on cold winter mornings had not amused him. It gave him a feeling of being exposed, observed, forced to social intercourse at a time of day when no sensible person wants to talk to anyone else.

Ann was the widow of an artillery colonel who'd disappeared at Dunkirk. She inhabited a desolate, rather menacing Gothic brick house on one of the side streets further up the river, toward Abingdon. There was a bus.

She opened the door herself, a thirty-five-year-old woman with short brown hair, clear blue eyes, boyishly slim with delicate, sensitive lines to her hips. From the start, he liked her friendly, playful manner. Side by side they walked up the dark, curving staircase. The house had three stories, and the two rooms she offered him were the only ones on the third floor; one had two windows on the garden.

She was standing in front of one of them, against the light, and he couldn't see her face; a faint, unusual scent reached him.

"I hope the rent isn't too high," she said. "I'm a widow, I have to put it up a bit."

He took the rooms and moved in a week later. She was the ideal landlady. Although she appeared to be home most of the time, it seemed as if she avoided unnecessary conversation. She had some friends who'd sometimes look in around tea time. The older ones were men, the younger ones were women. One was a very beautiful Armenian woman who'd sometimes arrive on horseback; she had a beautiful saddle horse she'd tie by the hedge, which made him nervous when he wanted to get in with his bike. He'd never had a very good relationship with horses.

Spring came early that year, and he acquired the habit of sitting in a folding chair in the garden, on the short green grass, writing themes and lab reports on a small typewriter that was the right size for his lap.

Day after day of the same calm, sunny weather. The lawn was cared for by an old gardener. He'd come once a week, carrying the lawn mower over one shoulder the way a soldier carries his rifle, with the rest of his tools in a gray canvas bag. He'd always have his tea in the kitchen, which was so old-fashioned that one half of it had an earth floor. At sunset, when it was time for Hans to gather up his things and leave the garden, the last light of the day illuminated long, straight contrails from east to west. It was the American strategic bombers returning from their exercise flights. Times were unsettled; the war in Suez had just ended, and the balance between the world powers was precarious. The strange red tracks were suspended above him like some kind of apocalyptic sign.

Ann would sometimes come into the garden, absent-mindedly taking a lawn chair and settling into a different corner, often half in the shade, her face turned away from him. There was intense contact between them, not really erotic, more like a common sensibility: the shadows of the clouds moved swiftly over the garden, and there was the same shiver in both of them.

One afternoon she asks him if he likes old-fashioned English cider. He doesn't really know, but it's probably something he should try. There is, she says, a shop down on Bow Street, a kind of wine cellar that's selling very cheap cider right now, six pounds for ten bottles. If he wants to take the opportunity, she can order for him, too. They'll deliver. Oh yes, he'd like to have ten bottles.

Almost in the same breath, she continues,

"This is a terrible old house, don't you think so, Hans? I shouldn't be living here. I should find something else. Have you noticed something menacing here?"

The strange thing is that without ever having wanted to admit it, or to formulate it, he has felt the same thing. The house closed in on you in a menacing way at night, with its peculiar protuberances and neo-Gothic gargoyles and its odd landings; it always seemed to be *on the watch*. It could look like a stage where the actors know that a play is about to begin but where the characters in the play don't know it as, unaware, armed only with the fact of their past existence, they walk onto the still empty stage.

"No, I hadn't noticed."

"Perhaps it's because you're so young, Hans. How old are you?"

"Twenty-three."

"You're rather sure of yourself, aren't you? You know what you want?"

"Sometimes."

"Often I can't sleep. It started during the war. You lie there in bed waiting for the alarm to go off. You never suffer from insomnia? Before an exam, perhaps?"

He thought, but he didn't think for long. He already had his answer ready.

"If you're uneasy and can't go to sleep some night, you can come to my room."

She did, that same night. A light spring rain was falling outside; he saw her enter the room, more as a shadow than as a solid figure. She sat down, surprisingly shy, on the edge of his bed. He knew rather than saw that she was dressed in a long, thin nightgown. She had a strong, unusual scent, something between musk and apples that had been left to shrivel in the bin for a very long time.

"Tell me, what are the girls like in Sweden?"

"I honestly don't know much about them."

The whole of the spring night was theirs, moist, warm, infinitely long. Faint smoke from smoldering branches in some fire in a garden, extinguished by the rain: everything was with them, and everything was theirs.

4

In Vienna, a heavy rain was falling. For him, it was late evening; always the same unpleasant feeling accompanying the change in time zones. Here there was a gray, autumnal afternoon. Smoke rose from the big oil refinery; it was raining heavily over the wide, boring river valley, the domed gasworks, with its basilica-like architecture, was as boring as ever and, in the slowly rising darkness, the airport bus found its way to Karl Lueger-Ring.

In former years, the commission had picked up its experts in a limousine at the airport. Undoubtedly, that had been more comfortable. They had discontinued that last year, in order "not to expose the experts to unwarranted risks of terrorist attacks." He sometimes wondered whether the reasons weren't economical. In the early '80s, people economized in the most unexpected places: Europe wasn't quite what it had been only five years before. The first few years he'd stayed at the Hilton. That was unnecessarily expensive (he'd always hated to throw money away, even other people's money, on something as simple and temporary as overnight accommodations).

Nowadays he always stayed with a friend at the Secretariat, Dr. Jacob Nussbaum. Nussbaum had a handsome, quiet apartment on one of the side streets on the outside of the Opernring, always with large bouquets of fresh-cut flowers standing on the heavy, dark tables, carefully changed and tended by a still beautiful, very quiet wife of Georgian ancestry. Nussbaum's youngest daughter was an antiquarian bookseller of the superior sort that only deals in very expensive books. He'd never met her, since he only had access to her quarters when she was away: a small two-room suite with a lingering smell of cigarette smoke, where the tortoise combs and the arsenal of expensive skin creams in the bathroom indicated that a coquettish, but perhaps not quite beautiful, woman was living there.

For several years back, the ritual had been very much the same. He'd always arrive the night before the meeting proper, and Nussbaum would catch him up on the latest intrigues. This took the form of a very simple dinner at the corner restaurant. Nussbaum had a habit of hanging what he referred to as his "professor's uniform," the chalk-striped suit he wore in the daytime—usually ordered and tailored during a visit to Cambridge, England—in his closet as soon as he returned from the Secretariat. He would present himself instead in corduroy jeans and a blue wool sweater at his usual corner table, where the wineglasses left ring-shaped marks as complicated as the structural formulae of a very large molecule, or perhaps as the diagrams of a very complex organization.

It was the kind of place where the ladies of the evening eat their early, slipshod dinner practically at the same table as the policemen, where elegant ladies and tired taxi drivers rub elbows at the same table. In other words: a place where you could speak without being disturbed. They'd always continued the evening over one or two whiskeys in Nussbaum's apartment, but that part had long been sacred to more private topics.

It was a conviction of Nussbaum's that the quality of international agencies had declined terribly in his lifetime. Probably he was right. Of course it was most painfully evident in the central U.N. organizations and similar places, where positions once filled by great, brilliant minds would now be filled by the *nepotism* of the Third World.

It wasn't worth moralizing over, Jacob considered. The international organizations were losing their original role in the world, were being reduced to propaganda institutions: loudspeakers, record players, xerox machines, for something that meanwhile was being produced somewhere else.

Actually, they were both superfluous. Their positions had long been mandarin posts, empty ceremonies: just as the government itself had become ritualized in ancient China at the end of a tottering dynasty, they lived in a world where everything that outwardly seemed to be of significance had been ritualized long ago.

Under the supervision of some twenty governments, they were developing and modifying control mechanisms for something which clearly could no longer be controlled. If they were simply to go public with their opinion that the proliferation of nuclear weapons could not be controlled, that no one could guarantee with any certainty what was going on in the subterranean factories of different countries, or what happened to uranium delivered to semi-industrialized underdeveloped countries, they'd become an embarrassment to the governments that paid them. There wasn't much more to be said.

Jacob paid the check which, even at today's prices, was modest. They trooped out into the rain. The Cathedral of St. Stephen disappeared upward into the mist. There weren't many people in the Cathedral Square.

They mounted carpeted marble stairs, and Jacob opened the door to his apartment carefully. His wife, a kind, quiet woman who wasn't much in evidence, seemed to have fallen asleep already. A few hyacinths stood silent and kindly against the night.

"I have the feeling there isn't much left," Jacob said,

"Of what?"

"Of what once made Europe, Europe."

The bells rang in one of the innumerable steeples, the rain splashed against cobblestones where Mozart once walked. They were in the city of Gustav Mahler, of Wittgenstein, but no longer did any ideas suggest themselves to this city.

"I've a hard time assessing that kind of question," Hasse said. "I come from a region, northern Scandinavia, which has never

94

really been part of Europe, or which always struggled against it. Scandinavia never really got into the swing of things."

"I think you're mistaken. Everything was founded on contradictions. Peripheral, exclusive border states with negative attitudes, like Sweden or Portugal, were important parts of the system. The system needed its counter images. Freedom *and* centralization. Renaissance *and* orthodoxy. I think you're wrong. Charles XII's soldiers at Narva, coarse warriors in a totalitarian war machine, were as important as Locke and Hume."

"Then Europe is just as much the health around Brunnbäck's Ferry as the crypt near here where the entrails of emperors rest in their copper vessels."

"Don't forget that we Jews are Europe, too. We're strangers, and without us this continent would hardly have existed. There's your great, your really interesting contradiction."

"Do you mind if I have another whiskey?"

"Not at all. It's a funny thing that I've often noticed: a Scandinavian will always have another drink when the conversation starts to get interesting."

"Really?"

"What I meant to say is that Europe, in the sense you experience it, in international agencies for example, is to a large extent nothing but an expression of Jewish universalism. What I'm referring to is the idea that there is a law which is more important, or more valid, than the will of the reigning monarch or popular opinion, which most often is rather primitive, and that this law applies to everybody. During the time of the Enlightenment this law disguises itself as reason, during the epoch of Liberalism it calls itself Human Rights. But the fundamental thing remains the same: the idea that having power doesn't mean that you have the right. God is *one*. At whom do you suppose that statement is directed?

"No one should make us believe that the strange Christian doctrine of the Trinity is the chief opposition. At the most, during the heyday of Hellenistic Judaism, there was the temptation of Gnosticism, the doctrine of two deities, one which repre-

95

sents values and one who has created the world that apparently contradicts them. The main enemy, though, is always something else. God is one; this concept doesn't constitute a challenge to the little deities of river valleys and springs, either. Nobody had been able to put an end to them anywhere in the world, the real small deities, the *lares*, the little puffs of wind through sacred woods, the black depths of old, slow rivers; all those things will catch your glance forevermore."

"But then where on earth *is* the chief opposition?"

"Can't you see that? The ancient temple towers, the pyramids, built on surfaces that diminish upward hierarchically, the kings in their terrible repose, hands resting on their knees, arms extended straight against the knees, or with crossed flails. The Baals, the ancient rugged towers, power disguised as divinity. The power that can build pyramids, putting blocks of stone on one another aided by a machinery of naked, emaciated human bodies. The state as God. That's the evil thing. *That's* the Other."

"Then you mean that European liberalism is fundamentally nothing but the Jewish creed?"

"Allowing for a certain oversimplification, yes, I'd say so. Without Jewish universalism and without Jewish belief in the permanence of values there is no room left for that kind of Europe. The only things to remain are the Baals, Lenin, the Nation, and this new trick called the State for Society."

"This is a new kind of argument for me, but if I've caught your meaning, the whole idea of citizens' rights is more than normally threatened in Europe at this time. But what do you have to say about Christianity? Doesn't the crazy Christian paradox of Grace have any meaning nowadays?"

"Christianity has a single weakness. But it is a big one. It isn't concerned with this world, but the next. It's the religion of ultimate crisis, originating during the darkest, bloodiest period of ancient history. Where it becomes valid, there isn't much left. I believe the day will come when it is valid. The day when the defeat is final. When the last big retreat from human values is already a fact. Until then, we need something more rational. Something that says no, that is still concerned with logic."

Hasse was silent. The tulips shone whitely in the room; some-

96

where a pipe gurgled in the substantial old *haut-bourgeois* five-story building. The rain had stopped. The darkness seemed to press on the window panes.

Hasse said: "I once had a friend, a *kind* of friend, who reminds me a great deal of what we've been talking about. He had a trait that's quite rare. He was able to establish a completely personal relationship with other people, but a relationship that was fundamentally completely impersonal. Do you understand what I mean?"

"Not quite. Well, yes, I think I know what you're talking about. He showed other people something that looked exactly like love or hate, but which actually wasn't either. He wanted to utilize something that looked like personal feelings to an impersonal end. Was he a politician?"

"No, he was a poet. At least when he was young. I have no idea what became of him later in life."

"Strangely enough, poets often have that trait. For approximately a hundred and fifty years, ruthless egoism has been encouraged in poets."

"Why?"

"So that we won't take them seriously. Then they might become norm givers. Note that during the classical period, poets had to be role models, paradigms of the moral virtues of their time."

"And we find that laughable."

"No one would accept that kind of irresponsibility in a professor of economics."

"My poet, if I may call him that, was actually dangerous. You know, there really are people who are *capable of anything.*"

"You're telling me. However, I don't mean extermination camps and torture. I'm talking about something much more mundane. An obvious, everyday kind of nihilism."

"That keeps increasing, you mean?"

"It's a social condition that nothing seems able to inhibit any longer. The only obstacle people try to erect in its path is fear of the state, disguised as something called 'solidarity.' That fear is much too brittle. Someone prepared for ultimate violence is not afraid of violence in others. And someone who himself doesn't have any values will not, in the last instance, be impressed by power. In brief: there's nothing, *nothing at all*, that stands between us and chaos anymore. The poets were the first to know it and to see the possibility of exploiting it. Baudelaire is no coincidence. He really *is* the secret agent of something new. . . ."

"The new emptiness that will open up behind the State God?"

"Something like that. Now tell me about your poet. What did he do to you?"

"It isn't easy to explain. We were in love with the same girl for a while. But he didn't need her any longer. And not for what she expected."

"Of course you were in love with each other as well?"

"Yes, but not manifestly."

"And he robbed you of that feeling, too?"

"Somehow I've always missed him. Or—perhaps I can put it in a better way. I had something in mind that disappeared with him. It feels rather as if I'd forgotten something very important that I should remember. And that I can't possibly remember any longer. Excuse me, but doesn't this start to sound totally impossible?"

"Do you mean, too *personal?*"

"Not at all. But it's starting to get difficult for exactly the opposite reason. A lot of things that happened when I was young, that I thought of as personal and private, are starting to look as if they belonged to a much larger, more public plot."

"This thing, behaving toward people as if you had a personal relationship with them, and then *not to want anything from them*, this subtle new way of being capable of anything, isn't that what every P.R. agency, every personnel director, is doing nowadays?"

"Personal relations disappear from the world along with the conviction of the existence of values?"

"That's what I believe."

"So people have to become more and more like one another?"

"Just like the poets. All of them—or almost all of them—after Baudelaire make the same claim of uniqueness, to having a personal voice. The paradoxical thing is that this very claim makes them so like one another that they are interchangable."

"Consequently a *vacuum*, emptiness once more. The same emptiness wherever you look."

"And nature abhors a vacuum."

"Above all, people abhor emptiness."

"It's getting late. What are you going to do when we finish tomorrow?"

"I thought I'd catch a late plane for Sweden. To Göteborg. There's something there I have a more personal interest in."

"Oh?"

"There's a small group of physicists in Göteborg who are interested in mapping out the energy resources of the planet. It feels a lot less sterile than what we're doing here."

"I'm sure you're right. You're still young enough to have hope in projects. Good night."

Without waiting for an answer, his host disappeared into darker, still quieter recesses of his vast apartment.

5

He himself slept uneasily in the elegant daughter's suite, with its foreign smells. The spring insomnia period was on its way. The dry heat in the room reminded him of his first marriage.

Those years—there were only seven of them—he lived first in Uppsala and then in Geneva; in Uppsala, in a small house on Krongatan, close to Physicum, and in Geneva in a succession of impersonal apartments kept for researchers, all of which seemed to have radiators that were much too hot, turned up much too far in the winter. For the duration of this marriage, he didn't possess a stick of furniture. There was never any question of children.

Annette, like him, was a physicist, a radiation physicist. It was easy for them to get jobs in the same place, something that was unusual at a time when researchers, almost as a matter of course, had got used to their wives' being in a completely different city from the one in which they themselves were living and working. There was no real explanation for the impersonal character of their relationship. They got along well; when they occasionally had guests and did the dishes afterward, they could carry on endless, funny conversations over the dishes. They saw each other rather clearly, but it's impossible that they were never quite conscious of what they saw.

It was impossible to explain why he'd married her. One of his ideas was that he'd done it because she didn't seem dangerous to him. >

Days when they were both home, they'd take turns making lunch. It always gave him a feeling of pleasurable joy to hear her rattling the dishes in the kitchen. At such times, the whole world was populated. If there was love between them, it consisted of such moments. To populate. To fill a room with sounds, steps, verbal exchanges.

The strange thing was that he could no more remember why he'd got divorced than he could remember why he'd married her. The last few years he had lovers, not very many, not very intense experiences; more and more, he traveled by himself; he was simply starting to break himself of her, rather as if it were a necessity demanded of him.

A personality, he thought, isn't quite the same thing as the line it cuts through life. It consists just as much of the choices it could have made (but never did) as of the choices it could not have made. Being married to Annette was, in the long run, incompatible with his personality. Not that it led to conflict but purely because that wasn't the way it was supposed to be.

What was strange about his decision to get divorced was that there was no particular moment when he made it; suddenly, one day, it was as obvious and irrevocable as death. Nothing between them had changed, only *this* had changed.

As a physicist, used to handling particles and their tracks in a cloud chamber, he'd always seen a profound similarity between the moment, the present moment, and death. Both represented the point from which you could no longer survey life, both were points in life where you no longer knew whether it would continue.

There was something profoundly disturbing and mysterious about this, since it was easy to establish that life consisted only of such moments.

100

Steeple bells tolled once again. With careful, shuffling steps (afraid to hit his toes against something unknown in the darkness of the room), almost like an old man, he went over to the window and pulled the curtain (which also smelled of cigarette smoke) to one side. His guess had been correct. It had started snowing, and the snow had changed even the sound of the bells. It must be very late for the season, he thought.

It struck him that he'd just described Jan as someone who used everybody who came his way. (Napoleon, Martin Buber once said, is a monster, because he has a personal relationship even with people who don't concern him in the least.)

Jan was *capable of anything* in accordance with the esthetics which in this world had replaced ethics. But how about himself? Wasn't he, too, capable of anything?

He was old enough now to have seen almost all the ages of women, from his own small American daughters to his ancient grandmother, who had died at the age of a hundred and one in the early '70s in an old people's home in Västmanland. He'd seen all those ages and knew how unbelievably short they were.

What had *he* robbed other people of, by not wanting anything from them? What would Annette have done if she hadn't lived with him for seven years?

Not a person, not even a car, moved through the new-fallen snow in the street. Tomorrow he'd have to explain to a number of politically appointed international bureaucrats that there was no longer any real possibility of supervising what their own nations were manufacturing and not manufacturing. And those experts and administrators, all in very similar suits, would listen very courteously, very sullenly, while they contemplated the most discreet and speedy way of divorcing him from his assignment. That was all right. He didn't need any more money than he was already making. It was time to devote himself to something different.

Before he went back to bed, which he hoped would be cooler by now, he thought:

Only when you feel welcome on earth is it possible to believe in God.

The huge emptiness in the middle of the night.

He arrived late in Göteborg, two days later, took the bus from Landvetter Airport, always strangely empty. Without seeing anything of the city, he ended up in the Lorensberg, a funny old hotel which, as he remembered it, used to be overrun with Finnish football players and field ornithologists, but which now seemed to have got quite a bit more expensive.

By that time it was already past midnight, and there wasn't much to do. Tomorrow he'd look up Professor Karl-Erik Eriksson to find out about his project: the mapping of earth's energy resources.

The water pipes in this hotel, he thought, make quite a different noise from the pipes in Vienna. Around me is Göteborg wrapped in night, a city I haven't seen properly since 1959. And I'm not seeing it now. Am I on the same planet? On the same time line, or on a similar one? The same rain that fell outside my window in Vienna, or perhaps it was lighter there, sea breezes, water on the twigs of trees glimpsed in the light from a street-lamp. The street below almost was empty of people. Two young men, apparently slightly intoxicated, were the only people in sight. They were dressed very much alike, in down jackets of a kind that hadn't been around in the late '50s. Had those boys even been born the last time he was in Sweden? Probably not. What kind of world were they living in? What were they thinking of?

For a moment he was bothered by a science fiction-like feeling of having landed on a strange planet. It was the moment when the travelers in the spaceship, while the dust from their landing settles, send out probes to see whether they can breathe the atmosphere, to examine the biological forms that life has taken on this distant planet. He felt a sudden terror, not so much of the old country as at the possibility of suddenly meeting himself out there. Thank God he was only staying for three days.

He wished he had access to the same ingenious contraption that travelers in spaceships usually did: an automated probe that could move imperceptibly along the streets, equipped with antennae and microphones, able to listen in on conversations, analyze tones of voice, take samples of people's voices and gestures. All of this to convince him that nothing had changed since the last time. Why is it so important to us that nothing should change when we leave a place?

It wasn't insomnia in the usual sense, more of a flaw, a small scar, a spot where his sleep had broken once and for all and could no longer be repaired. It was between three and four in the morning. He called it "the white hole." He knew exactly when and how it had occurred.

It was that summer at Oxford.

He'd left Ann in the beginning of July, just as the term ended. He'd moved out in a big hurry and of course he'd forgotten the cider bottles, which were probably still standing there in the cellar dust, unless someone had found them in the meantime. The last few weeks it had been completely impossible to talk to her. She replied in a strange, preoccupied manner, as if something else always had her attention. She seemed to be living in incomprehensible terror.

Many years passed before he found out, in a roundabout way, from one of her student boarders, that she'd ended up in a mental hospital that same fall, that she was in a bad way, quite apathetic. He didn't know what had happened to her after that.

For years afterward he experienced it as a betrayal, and the empty spot in the middle of his sleep somehow represented this betrayal, rather as if she had, for all time to come, taken a piece of him with her when she disappeared into her labyrinth.

Fundamentally, he didn't object to it: it was a form of penance and an insurance against changing, dissolving into nothingness.

Someone who has that kind of gap in his sleep will acquire something like a secret life over the years.

The sleepless hour *was* completely sleepless. It had the shadowless clarity of total, absolute sleeplessness. A strange, rediscovered desert city in Ecuador or a high plateau in the Alps in the middle of the day: glittering snow, relentless light, each individual hiker visible against the snow for miles off, a small black dot. Perhaps one of those science-fiction planets that has two suns. When one sinks red on the horizon, the other, menacing, blue

103

and cold, is already rising on the opposite horizon, creating a new, false dawn which in some strange way enlarges new details, shows cracks in rocks that looked quite smooth just before.

His sleep injury was a magnifying lens.

He might start thinking of someone he hadn't seen for decades, a schoolmate he hadn't seen since elementary school, an assistant with thin, nickel-framed glasses and a dry, matter-of-fact voice with whom he had worked in Stanford one winter many years ago. All these people suddenly came alive, posing riddles he couldn't solve.

There was always a limit: the only thing you could see of your life was the past, and the past formed a dense, mysterious forest petrified by the moment.

But the moment itself was always completely empty.

There was no possibility of differentiating between the moment and death.

If he mishandled his injury, the result was that he would lie there sleepless until morning and then have a terrible day with a headache that lasted far into the afternoon. One way to mishandle it was to make too much of it. If you just treated it as the most natural thing in the world, at about ten minutes past four, you'd feel the landscape, parched from shadowless and dry clarity, start to fill again with the cool waters of sleepiness. The mild rain of tiredness filled the rocky and desiccated brook beds, and suddenly you were back among ordinary people: you slept, deeply as a child.

There were different things you could do in the emptiness. The important thing was to endure its unrelenting light, its absence of shadow.

At home he was careful never to use this mysterious hour for work. Thinking about your problems was dangerous. You'd always find new ones. Reading novels was impossible. There was always the risk that the novel would prove so interesting that you'd go on reading past four o'clock.

In the sleeplessness of hotel rooms, he'd acquired the habit of reading telephone books. They were at once innocent and interesting. And they were always handy, like the hotel Bible. For some reason, he always avoided that scrupulously.

104

But telephone books were fun. It was possible to see that there was a family in Boston called Granquist (Robert and Jo Ellen), that the watchmakers in New Delhi were concentrated in a surprisingly small area at the city center, that Houston had more Olsens than Olssons, that Zürich was full of people called Dürrenmatt, but that the real Dürrenmatt, that is to say the great playwright, was not in the phone book. Was he dead, perhaps?

It was possible to see the statistical population distribution, or at least to get a fair idea of it; you could see to what extent people were interchangeable, how far entropy had advanced. And you could see, like the misty particle tracks in a cloud chamber, the tracks of some past that no longer existed. The Polish names in the Chicago phone book, the Lettish and Estonian names in Newark, the last traces of General Vlassov's Ukrainian rebel army in the Sydney telephone book, such as Ukrainian grocery stores, Ukrainian hairdressers.

The Göteborg phone book was heavy and closely printed, the way he remembered Swedish telephone books. It was easy to find Professor Karl-Erik Eriksson. (He lived out in Kungsbacka and some time tomorrow Hasse would call his office at Chalmers; they'd already arranged the time.) Hans-Åke Ohlsson was the name of a pianist and of two bricklayers, and Mats Furberg was a university teacher.

Of course he found her: Ann-Marie Nöhme. It was her he'd been looking for the whole time; there she was, in what appeared to be a suburban house; there was no letter after the house number, and it seemed plausible that it should be her, especially since there was the title "opera singer" after her name.

The discovery made him sit straight up in his bed. He'd have had palpitations if he hadn't felt sure that it would be a ridiculous way to behave. He wondered what his red-haired wife at home in Cambridge would say if she could see him now.

But that wasn't what agitated him. What made him sit very stiff and straight up in bed, still with the heavy phone book in his lap, staring at the wall, was something which only slowly crossed his mind.

For years he'd been sure that Ann-Marie Nöhme was dead. She'd died from a viral infection. Had he changed time lines, the way time travelers sometimes did? Had he returned to the wrong world, one that was only approximately the right one?

In his treacherous memory he saw her, small and thin in a rough-textured nightgown, sitting as stiffly upright as he was doing now, in a distant hospital bed.

But if she wasn't dead, then she must be alive.

5   Those Vanished Without a Trace

1

On the east side of Place de la République in Dakar, under the pleasantly shadowed arcades, the hangouts of news vendors and shoeshine men, there are several banks to choose from. At nine or a quarter past, when the customers start to collect in front of the marble counters and the ceiling fans start to move, a few papers fluttering up from the green bundles of documents, they are pleasingly cool.

Passably shaved, in a passable cotton suit from one of the storekeepers in the Medina one of the Lebanese tailors found there, in a long row, with old-fashioned sewing machines that sound like crickets in the afternoon heat, I'm finding my way into the Crédit Lyonnais.

It took eight whole days to get there from Ziguinchor. The first day had been consumed in getting the jeep. The second I had mostly spent changing and repairing the right rear tire; I don't think I made more than eighty kilometers. The third day I bought a new inner tube in a nice little outdoor repair shop in Diakoye Banga. The man who put the new tube in the tire broke off from time to time to pour cold water from a wooden dipper over the shoulders of his two little boys, who were playing in the shadow of a large gray baobab. The road up toward Bathurst was good for the time of year. The only sensational thing was a truck with camels that had overturned on a curve with bigger than usual potholes, spilling its contents over the meager bush in the bend of the road. The animals, their necks broken, were hanging here and there like some kind of fruit. Clouds of black flies over their spilled guts, their long, beautiful legs broken at odd angles, a few vultures flapping above it all. A picture that would have captivated Eugène Delacroix and a bad omen for me. There was a heavy stink of putrefaction for several kilometers downwind; the scene brought a strange exultation in its wake. It was a kind of farewell. A warning wing beat so close to me that I could feel the air current.

The passage through Gambia across the bridge can be very slow if you don't pay the customs men, and I knew that. I passed them the number of bills I considered correct. It's important not to pay too much; then they get really suspicious. As it was, they just glanced at my pair of simple, rough suitcases in the back seat. They aren't much to look at, and this time there wasn't anything interesting inside them, either.

Late at night on the eighth day I arrived in Dakar, with almost no money, after having bought gas for the last time in Thiès. I realized that I wouldn't get into a hotel without paying a deposit, since I was dirty and unshaven.

After some very tiring wandering about in the Medina, in the large, new Medina, I found a house where I've known the whole family for a long time. I spent the night in the small whitewashed room with four boys, all brothers, of whom the oldest was eighteen and the youngest five. They rolled quietly on their mats in their sleep, talking Wolof in dreams to which I had no access. For a moment, I forgot the pain of no longer knowing who I was or where I was going.

The first of the local roosters woke me at five, and I washed in the yard as soon as I could, since I knew that the crush around the only water faucet on the block would be great as early as six o'clock. I left my last bill on the kitchen table, under a sticky bottle of sesame oil, and stole away. All the small boys stood around, cheering on my decrepit jeep until I got it started.

On the stroke of nine I was in the Consul General Koch's office. He was in, he recognized me as soon as I managed to make my way past the secretaries. He scrutinized me with large, blue, affable old man's eyes. His face bore the traces of a long time spent in the country; he had the characteristic, almost scar-like planes in his forehead and on his cheekbones that you acquire after forty years of African sun. He was the oldest Scandinavian in Dakar, originally from Denmark. He'd been sitting there when de Gaulle's warships fired on the harbor. Koch knew everyone and was beloved of captains and Swedes in the export business for his pleasant little dinners. He had a small hut, for swimming, on the island of N'gor, where he used to invite friends and business contacts to swim and to rest on the dazzling white sand Sunday afternoons. I myself had been invited there a few times in the late '60s and early '70s.

110

His friendly, generous spirit was strongly reminiscent of the type of old grocer who keeps a store in a Copenhagen basement.

"Hello, it's been a while," Koch said.

"Yes, when was it?" I said.

Five, six years.

"You've got business in Dakar?"

"It's a bit complicated," I said to gain time.

"By the way, I just remembered, I've got a letter for you," Koch said. "There was a boy with an envelope, and the whole thing happened in such a rush that my secretary never had a chance to find out where he came from. He was gone before I could tip him, even. I'll get it for you."

Deliberately, he opened the heavy door of his safe and handed me a thin, white envelope.

"Have you got a paper knife?" I asked, trying to hide my nervousness.

The only thing in the envelope was a check. The amount was satisfactory. It was for more than what my store and my boat and my other assets had ever been worth.

I took a good look without removing the check from its envelope. The consul peered at me. His bookcase was full of the oddest publications: *Swedish Shipping List* in its blue binding, as blue as the sea; the *State Calendar* in a red one; three books on Sweden by Gullers, the photographer; a lot of back issues of a magazine I wasn't familiar with but which was evidently called *Sweden Now.* An old-fashioned fan with mahogany blades dangled from the ceiling.

"It's okay?" Koch asked.

"Not too bad," I said. "You see, I've sold my boat and the store. I'm moving back home."

"That's quite something. You got fed up?" the consul asked.

It was impossible to tell what he did or didn't know.

"Times are bad," I said.

"That's true, yes, damn inflation. But I thought you had quite a few tourists down there nowadays. I hear from the Hotel Diola that they're overbooked with Club Med groups all the time."

"I have various reasons," I said.

"I understand," the consul said. "Do you have a passport?"

I took my passport out of my inside pocket. The cover was badly dog-eared.

He took it judiciously, removed a ten-franc note that had insinuated itself between two of the leaves and which I thankfully stuck in my breast pocket.

"Dear me, this ran out in 1975," he said worriedly. "Do you want me to make you out a new one? You'd like me to do that, wouldn't you? Let's see—you were born in Högalid Parish, May 17, 1936?"

"Will it take long?" I asked.

"You can have it in half an hour."

"Wonderful."

"Would you like a small whiskey while you wait?"

"Yes, please."

"So you're planning to settle back in Sweden?"

"I don't know. I'm going there to see. I'll decide later."

"Another drink?"

The consul, generous, but also sensitive, was beginning to realize that I didn't have much to say about my plans. As yet.

"No, thanks. It's a bit early in the day for me. I'm going to the bank."

"It's closed today. A holiday."

"But you're open?"

"I go by the Swedish calendar."

"Then Swiss Air will be closed, too?"

"All the airlines. Are you in that much of a hurry?"

"I've had a small difference of opinion with the governor in Casamance. Right now, it's the position of the authorities that I should leave the country."

"That's quite something. What the hell have you been up to?"

"Nothing in particular. I helped two gentlemen into Guinea-Bissau who were anxious to go there. Something must have happened to them on the other side."

"It wasn't a terribly propitious moment, I'm afraid. From a foreign policy point of view."

"I realized that afterward. We don't read newspapers that much in Casamance, you know."

In his blue old man's eyes I saw a sudden expression of pity. There's hardly anything that irritates me as much as when people start to show that they pity me.

"You're coughing a lot."

He was right. I'd been coughing continuously since I came in.

"It's the air conditioning. You know what it's like. You come from the hot street into an ice-cold room, and then it's all the dust. I drove up yesterday, you know."

"But you really don't look well. Do you want me to get you a good doctor?"

He already had his hand out to get his address book.

"No, of course not," I said. "It's nothing, really. I'd like to call around and find a hotel room."

"Hôtel de la Paix downtown is dark and a bit uncomfortable but cosy. Then you've got the Teranga, with all the businessmen and diplomats and people from the international organizations for underdeveloped countries, and tourists. Do you want me to have my secretary call them?"

"How long do you suppose I can stay? Before something else happens?"

"Over the weekend, I'd guess. Hardly more than a week. It was an unusual mark of confidence, I'd say, that they let you travel on your own."

"I suspect they had their reasons."

"Would you like to borrow some money until tomorrow?"

"That'd be great. Can I have a couple of thousand?"

"Take four. The Teranga's gotten to be expensive, like everything else."

The jeep, beat up, covered with dust, with one headlight more or less hanging loose, seemed somewhat out of place among the long, blue-black limousines outside the Teranga in the shadow of the canopy. A couple of elegantly uniformed porters took charge of my luggage. The desk clerk treated me with respect. They had experience with eccentric motoring tourists. I turned over my spanking new passport, and that didn't raise any eyebrows, either. The girls at the desk were completely engrossed in fussing with their hairdos.

The room was large and pleasant. Through the open balcony

door I heard the heavy, massive sound of the South Atlantic swell. My cough echoed in the shower. It didn't want to stop. It wasn't bad to be able to have a really good scrub with hot water for the first time in weeks.

Wrapped in a dry towel, I lay down on the bed. Slowly, my cough subsided. I realized I must have been quite tired.

Tomorrow I'd go to the bank, walk in under the slowly rotating fans at the Crédit Lyonnais, find my way among the marble counters, and cash a check for five hundred thousand French francs.

The rest was a riddle, and for some reason it no longer frightened me.

2

At about the same time, Hasse was on his way by cab toward the western outskirts of the city. He had four hours and was on his way to carry out a very private experiment.

The city looked shabbier than he remembered it, more worn and more impersonal. People looked to be in a hurry, and everyone was dressed markedly alike in down jackets. He had no memory of Swedes looking so *uniformed* in the '50s. Most of the people he saw were in their teens or twenties. Strikingly few old people, and very few children. He felt old.

The meeting in Vienna had been typical: just as he'd expected. In the ordinary meeting room, with the peculiar green glass cages of the interpreters at his back, he'd seen delegates and experts leaf through his report, and he'd made the customary summing up.

The gist of it was that the whole project of which his paper formed a part was largely unrealizable; everyone listened attentively without making any comments. Just as he expected, the rest of the debate focused on questions of procedure.

The only sign that he'd actually said anything was that the British delegate, Professor Michael Gardiner from King's College, Cambridge, came up to him during the break (they were

114

surrounded by a visiting class of schoolchildren chaperoned by a small, round, bald teacher, who loudly explained the tasks of the Commission to children not particularly willing to listen) to discuss some statistical data about West African uranium deposits. Wasn't that a startlingly large figure? No, it came from a French source.

That whole afternoon in Vienna he'd fought a feeling of increasing meaninglessness. Not even the thought that he'd soon be back in Cambridge, Massachusetts, with his red-haired witch and his two exemplary daughters offered any real stimulation.

The same strange emptiness was with him this morning in Göteborg, two days later. Perhaps it was simply fatigue. Or surprise that his memory had been so faulty.

He reminded himself that when he was younger, he used to feel something like this after a bad cold, an emptiness caused by fatigue, like wind blowing through the empty windows of an abandoned cottage.

They entered the narrow streets around the West Hospital, and he asked the driver to stop one block short. He wanted to walk the last stretch.

What had to be the very first winter snow had already started falling; it fell very peacefully in big flakes, one after another, and he marched determinedly down the street. For a moment, it was quite impossible to comprehend what he was doing.

But the snow kept falling calmly.

3

When I woke up the soft darkness had already fallen. I pulled on my cotton suit, tied one of my few ties around the collar of a shirt that had once been elegant, shaved, and took the elevator to the dining room.

The quiet little musician was playing a native string instrument with a soft, complaining tone. As yet there were very few people in the dining room. A large table of Frenchmen were evidently doing business. A small, extremely elegant, very dark-haired but white lady, who had to be an Arab, perhaps Lebanese, was drinking lemon tea from a glass with well modulated, softly acrobatic movements.

I'd just got the menu when a new little group entered. It was a blond girl in shirt and jeans, a bit broad across the beam, and two young men in similar shirts and jeans, both of them with big blond beards. They sat down at the table next to mine, and it didn't take me a second to realize that they were actually speaking Swedish.

"The per diem is one hundred ninety-five," the girl said, very decidedly, as if it were the end of a long discussion.

"But then it's higher in Liberia," the bigger beard said.

"What the hell do you expect. The hotel in Liberia is a lot more expensive."

"No wonder, when they have an indoor skating rink at the hotel," the other guy said.

"But isn't there a cheaper hotel in Dakar?" the girl asked.

"I'm sure there are lots of fleabags downtown, but I'm sure they smell of piss and old malaria."

"The worst thing is that they don't speak English in those small hotels. You've got to speak French. You can't even book a telephone call if you don't speak French. It's imperialism."

"At any rate, there won't be much left over," the girl said.

"It's rotten," one of the guys said. "The per diem is the only thing that's stainless."

They were a little hard to place. They weren't quite tourists, and of course not businessmen either. Journalists, perhaps? One problem was "stainless per diem." I simply didn't understand it. It must have something to do with the Welfare State.

"Hello," I said.

"Well, hi there," the older one said.

The girl looked at me with some suspicion. I had the feeling that she examined my tan and my cotton suit. Good thing I'd remembered to shave, I thought.

"You aren't a tourist," the girl said.

"No," I said. "But I've worked some in tourism."

"So you're living in Dakar," the younger one said.

There was a faint note of almost clinical distancing in his "so."

But there was also a note as if he were well within his rights, putting such a personal question.

"I've lived in Senegal for many years," I said. "But not in Dakar. A bit further south, in the Casamance district. My name is Jan Bohman, by the way."

"My name is Birgitta Liljekvist," the girl said.

The name of the older guy was Bosse Jansson, and the younger one, who seemed very sure of himself, was called Hasse Frid.

"We're here to reconnoiter for a documentary program for Swedish television," Bosse Jansson said. "Hasse is a reporter, and Britta's a script girl. I'm a producer."

"So you're out there filming all day?"

"No. We're just reconoitering. We find locations, that sort of thing. The filming won't start until the fall."

"You'll have to forgive me," I said. "When I was in Stockholm last, TV had just started. There were trial transmissions from Stockholm University."

"Have you been here that long," the girl said, sounding even more suspicious than Bosse Jansson had just before.

"I like it in Africa. Or I have liked it. Now I'm on my way home, anyway."

"You know there's an airline strike," said Hasse, warningly. He had something of the schoolteacher about him.

"Where? In Dakar?"

"No, in Sweden. The air-traffic controllers are out, it's a big strike of white-collar workers. For a week, no planes have been able to land."

"That's quite something," I said. "There never used to be things like that in the '50s. Or were there? Only France had strikes in those days. But you can fly Air France to Paris and take the train, can't you?"

No one seemed to have any comment on that kind of proposal. I decided to get to Air France as early as possible the next day.

Britta would have been a beautiful girl if she hadn't had such sharp, close-set eyes.

"So how do you like Senegal?" she demanded.

"I like it. It's a friendly country, very democratic by African

117

standards. They have their problems, but there's relative harmony. And the population consists of some of the most intelligent peoples in Africa: Diola, Wolof, Serers . . ."

"So you mean that peoples have different intelligences," the girl said. She didn't seem to approve of it.

"We think it's kind of gruesome here," she added.

"Why?"

"Colonialism is still rampant. Just think of French. Even public places have French names."

"But then Canada would be colonial, too?"

"I guess we see things a bit differently," Hasse said, very composedly. "But you have to admit that there's a high degree of exploitation here?"

"Depends what you mean. If you compare with what the new upper classes are doing in Guinea-Bissau and in Tanzania or with their opposite numbers in Uganda, then Senegal becomes an idyll."

Hasse thought for a long time.

"You're comparing colonial conditions with new republics that haven't yet found their political form. It's not really fair."

"There were often articles in the Swedish press in the late '30s dealing with the Third Reich," I said, "stating that it was unfair to attack a state that hadn't yet found its political form."

"Listen, don't you think we should order?" Britta asked.

Their way of dealing with the headwaiter was completely wrong. They insisted on treating him with a kind of camaraderie which probably made him furious, since of course he was a very experienced and accomplished professional, proud to be in charge of the Teranga dining room. They asked about everything, as if they suspected it of being poisoned, and they were never satisfied with just one answer. Of course he got tired of it and asked if he might return later.

He came over to my table, and I ordered a pilaf and a glass of ice water. Those Swedes had a funny mixture of childishness and suspicion which amused me. Mostly the suspicions.

While they waited for what they might want to eat when the headwaiter at last, sullenly, returned to their table, they each ordered whiskey. The beautiful Lebanese woman was still sitting alone at her table with her lemon tea. I wondered to myself whether she might be waiting for someone. There were more people in the dining room by now.

Two gentlemen by the door, in very well-pressed white mantles, had been sitting still for such a long time that I started to suspect that it was me they were there to keep an eye on. That might well be the case. They were drinking glasses of tea and looking very determinedly into their respective books each time I looked in their direction. Plainclothes policemen would act that way. The Swedish TV people no longer seemed to be interested in me.

"What's Sweden like nowadays," I asked. "Apart from being on strike?"

"There's a conservative government."

"With high taxes and prices."

"Quite a bit of unemployment."

"What do people talk about nowadays?" I asked. "In my youth people talked about the danger of a third world war."

"People still do," Hasse said.

"Not so much among ordinary people. It's mostly the intellectuals who're into it."

"Apart from that it's mostly this tax jippo," the photographer said.

(There were at least two words I didn't understand at all, "jippo" and the strange way of using "into.")

"You're coughing a lot," the girl said.

"Dust," I said. "I drove up from Casamance. You get a lot of dark red laterite in your lungs."

"To me it sounds like chronic bronchitis."

"Yes, well, perhaps I'd better get some sleep," I said.

I put the check on my hotel bill. The two well-dressed gentlemen were still sitting down by the door, were still drinking minuscule amounts from their tea glasses and looking down into their books. The young people from Swedish TV were still sitting at their table, having a lively discussion. Perhaps they were discussing me? I liked them, and at the same time, they seemed very foreign. Cousins from a related world.

But it was almost impossible to pinpoint what the foreignness consisted of.

Only when I was in the elevator did I discover that the Leba-

119

nese lady was there, too. She looked a little bit older close up. Her eyebrows were heavily made up, and she wore an almost inch-wide gold bracelet on her left wrist, which was very brown.

Was she a refugee? Or perhaps the daughter of one of the old business families in Dakar? Like all such women she looked energetically into a corner, especially after the rest of the passengers, a group of older Frenchmen, got out on the fourth floor.

"You should be a bit more careful."

"About my cough, you mean? Oh, it's just a bit of dust in my bronchial tubes."

"About your cough, too. It'll be ready in a few days, by the way."

I was so surprised that when the automatic door opened, I automatically stepped out. Impossible to find her again, impossible to question her further.

4

What is it that keeps us in motion?

Not seldom, the fear that the bitterness of the past will catch up with us. The bitterness over all the things that never got done, bitterness over all missed opportunities. Bitterness at being who you are, and still not more like yourself.

I've always had a tendency to break off conversations too soon. How did I become who I am? How did I end up in Ziguinchor for so many years? Because it was a place that didn't demand much of me?

But that's wrong. More was demanded of me there than would have been at home. At home I could have gone on writing the same kinds of poetry books, varying them slightly (and they would have said that now the poet has started down *a new path*, and it wouldn't have been the truth), sitting in restaurants and cultivating contacts, winning prizes and grants. It's quite impossible to imagine what it would have been like. Everything turns dark when I try to imagine it. My poetry would have looked like *poetry* today.

In order not to betray art I had to betray it.

If I really look back, look around among those who were truly gifted, more than normally gifted, in my youth, among the poets, among the painters, those who had something new to say, it strikes me that the best ones didn't stay. They became something else. A couple of the painters ended up in mental institutions or in facilities for alcoholics. Other people took their ideas and became famous as a result. Destroyed by drink, dissolved by narcotics, they died off or disappeared into institutional labyrinths. Some simply chose to become trivial. Journalists on Norrland newspapers. Minor functionaries.

I hardly know what those who stayed were really like. I knew so few of them in the late '50s, and then I lost touch. Those who survive aren't the ones who survive.

Surviving is also an art.

I really wonder what the Lebanese lady might have meant? Or did I just dream that I was talking to her and she asked me to wait and be patient?

When I first went to France, in 1961, the pretext was that I was going to write articles for *Stockholms-Tidningen*. There were a few, but by and by the paper started to return everything. Either I started to lose touch with my own language, or else I got careless. Besides, they changed the cultural editor in the meantime.

I was a waiter in Cannes for a whole year and lived in an apartment house, above a dressmaker's. I remember the sound of the sewing machines quite well. They sounded like crickets. It was mostly older women who did the sewing; they never returned my greeting when I said good morning to them.

The owner of the restaurant was a stingy, generally unpleasant Greek, Monsieur Christos Morelatos. He used to sit at the cash register all day, sunk in a kind of Byzantine ritual staring, empty and alert at the same time.

From a friend who was a student from Lyon I soon learned how to make a little on the side, acting as a gigolo to middle-aged American ladies. I never dared try the really old ones. I never succeeded in making a big kill.

But I learned a few things about myself.

For example, if you're a waiter who goes out with a rich, not terribly attractive American lady, all the other waiters recognize that you're a waiter making extra money as a gigolo. For the most part, I liked the American ladies surprisingly well. They wanted so little from me.

For some reason, it's always been important to me that people shouldn't want too much from me. It was important to me not to have too much of an impact on other people. That was the bad thing. I always wanted to damage my own possibilities, to rob them of reality.

Of course I also tried the other, homosexual, love at that time. It brought less money. It was mostly Englishmen who were interested, and of course there were those North Africans. I never liked them. They didn't belong.

I was amused by the funny mirror effect that appears when you go to bed with someone of the same sex. You return to your own world, so to speak, although from a different direction; you see the world you just left in a new light. Women always retain their mystery. I can understand why philosophers have always been more interested in boys than in girls. Girls are theology, boys are philosophy.

I must have written a number of sonnets in French that year in Cannes, without being able to hold on to them. Lots of poems disappeared, for the simple reason that I couldn't return to some rented rooms to collect my things. The back rent was too large. I must have lost more poems that way than I ever published in Sweden.

It's hard to think back on it. Nowadays I don't believe I could get even four lines together. It's finished. It's empty when I look in that direction, and I don't know why.

Most of my French sonnets were homosexual eulogies to a young Senegalese I became acquainted with at that time. His name was René Bethio, and he was of course typical of the period in his interest in anticolonial thinkers, *Négritude*, and Sartre's philosophy. A tall, handsome, rather stern student of about twenty-five, who claimed that he'd studied at the Sorbonne and substituted at various provincial lycées. His rooms, which were always a little better than mine, were full of books. He was a great reader, René Bethio. But he always used to have a small drum. He taught me that North Africa, Moslem Africa, has string instruments, while Africa south of the Senegal River has the drum. His drum was very small. He beat on it lightly with his fingertips while he recited his poems. It was often called *Négritude* at the time. His poems were often very good.

They often dealt with ancestors with lion masks and with Marx's theory of surplus value, practically in the same stanza. Aimé Césaire was important then.

His optimism, even his *Négritude* were, in some strange way, maintained by his being abroad. He'd never have been able to keep the same feeling deep in Africa. There the days are long and gray. A schoolteacher under the green arches in Casamance hardly feels Africa vibrate inside him. The sky can be warm and gray there: the water like mercury.

Like almost everything for us at that time, Africa, too, was theatrical.

Be that as it may, the next year I followed René to Senegal. We were both threatened with expulsion due to some small problems we had. Petty theft, things like that. He showed me his home district, the little white villages around Thiès. We drove around in a beat-up old Renault accompanied by two of his friends, drinking coffee in the silent, white-washed, quiet cafés, where old men would sit engrossed in pious texts or in detective stories while a slow fan moved on the ceiling.

This was already an older Senegal, one there isn't much left of now. For a while we were living together outside Thiès; René worked as a schoolteacher, and I was trying to write what could have been my next Swedish poetry book. It didn't work.

For some reason, René became more and more introverted, more and more bitter. It had nothing to do with our relationship. That was impersonal and happy.

It was something in his home district that poisoned him. The Africa he returned to wasn't the same Africa as the Africa of the French cafés. *Négritude* was grayer here, a rustling of dry leaves in a stubborn wind over Cap Vert, centuries having vanished without a trace, and a small monkey chattering outside the light house. No longer any ancestors with lion masks.

He just got terribly uncommunicative and depressed.

I left him and ended up in Dakar, where I worked for a year in the office of a factory in the Free Trade Zone that made burlap bags for peanuts. René committed suicide six months later. He couldn't take the return home. That's the way it was. There was no other explanation.

What I really wanted to talk about was homosexuality and what it's meant to me. Mirror image. A state of peace in between states. A zone that's neither day nor night.

But still full of the pain of creation.

5

Women are always frightening in a different way, because women are always riddles.

The next day, with my money in a French bank account and a promise from Air France to call around one about my flight (there was still some kind of strike in Sweden, and I started thinking seriously of staying in Paris to see how the situation would develop), I grabbed a towel and took the elevator down to the Teranga's swimming pool.

The Lebanese lady was there. A big, black lifeguard with a heavy beard was teaching her to swim: she abandoned herself to the water with delighted little cries when he removed the guiding boathook he'd held in front of her. It was hard to estimate her age. She might be a teenager or a twenty-year-old. She wore her black hair up, in little braids.

Perhaps it wasn't altogether necessary to estimate her age.

I settled under an umbrella and watched her. She knew very well that I was there: I could tell from the way she was stretching her neck. She had a very beautiful, very narrow, very tanned back. Had she arrived recently? Was she Christian or Moslem?

My cough returned. It puzzled me: there no longer seemed to be any outward cause for it. I no longer smoked; I hadn't swallowed anything the wrong way; there was no reason for me to cough. And still I did, long, suffocating, dry coughing spells.

I was so preoccupied by my coughing spell that I didn't notice

124

her until she was sitting in the chair next to mine. Something was obviously going wrong. I was getting sick.

Your body always opens itself to something. The body opens itself to hate or to love. And the whole time this sense of how fast your life is passing.

And of how slowly the curtain rises.

"You wouldn't happen to have the right time," said the young lady.

6

The blackened snow of March, already sooty, only visible in drifts behind the shelters at the bus stops. The dog's old bones, which it had got for a Christmas present, sticking up from a snow bank behind a bush three houses down the street.

Ann-Marie Nöhme was deep in a state that was typical of her in spring.

She'd remain standing at the sink, completely absorbed in a single spot of leftover yolk on a plate. Its concentrated repulsiveness then turned into the picture that conferred depth on the world. Its very unwillingness to disappear, to let itself be scraped off the edge of the plate, even with her nail, was typical of the kind of *stickiness* that separates the being (as Sartre would put it) from nothingness. The kitchen, the whole house in fact, had a characteristic silence on such mornings. She didn't like it. She, who never otherwise was particularly paranoid, could get a feeling of being supervised, without knowing who might be "supervising" her.

The dogs, two boisterous Labradors, were sometimes let out into the yard, where they chased from one dirty snow bank to another. They'd throw themselves against the gate every time somebody walked by, always with the same merry, territorial fury.

She liked it pretty well. Fundamentally, she'd always liked fences, southern houses with high, white walls with glass embedded in the top. She was one of those people who don't always answer the phone, even if it keeps ringing.

She considered that she had a right to herself which no one was allowed to violate.

For the third time some character in a heavy cashmere winter coat was walking down the street, with a Burberry hat pulled down over his forehead. Probably a salesman.

What on earth could he find to spy on?

Sometimes she'd feel a sudden abhorrence of men. It stretched from her father—the last years in particular, when you'd find traces of feces on his sheets and in his underpants in the morning, to all those sticky-seeming orchestra types who nowadays would sometimes tag along after the rehearsal. This was the kind of day when the world was sticky.

Its stickiness made it real. Often, especially at times when she wasn't doing any serious singing, and especially right before her period, she had the feeling that this stickiness was what kept her attached to sensuality. Sensuality was reality. Basically, however, it was also a way of avoiding contact with the world, a contact that might drive her mad, or kill her.

What it consisted of she didn't know. She only knew that from childhood, she was used to fighting one terror with another.

It was time to take the dogs for a walk. They knew it and danced around the hall, scratching with swift claws at the door panel, already hopelessly ruined. Moments like these she saw them as tormentors.

Hasse, who by now had had time to walk around the block twice, had a certain respect for those dogs he could hear through the door. The fear of getting his fingers chewed up, and perhaps also the fear that she might be married to someone really unpleasant, stopped him from simply ringing the doorbell.

She solved the problem for him by coming out, carelessly dressed in a fur jacket and blazing red pants, the dogs dancing around her. She had gotten so much heavier; the witch-like trait, which had always been there, was intensified; her hair shifted toward reddish-blond and lay rather heavily on the collar of her jacket.

There was a chance she'd recognize him; he both feared it and entertained a wild hope that she would. They met, barely a yard

126

apart, and she looked at him dismissively. They had already walked past one another when he turned and asked,

"Excuse me, is this the way to the West Hospital?"

"Not quite," she said, absent-mindedly and quickly, walking on as if nothing had happened.

"But I really need to get there," Hasse said.

"Are you ill or something?" she looked at him long and disapprovingly. The dogs sniffed his right glove, alert but quiet. He hadn't changed.

"Not I. Just my shadow. And not incurably."

Was this a madman she had encountered? For a moment, they were enclosed in a kind of bubble of understanding and nonunderstanding, of recognition and nonrecognition, where neither counted. Hasse felt a very slight dizziness; some crazy magpies circled over the suburb at a hundred meters.

"I work for a pharmaceutical company," he said. "I'm on my way there to demonstrate a new method of anesthesia for the hospital management."

"I assume," she said, in her coldest, clearest soprano voice, piercing him with blue eyes that had turned colder over the years, "I assume that it will be of use to someone at any rate."

He noticed that while most Swedes in the street and in stores nowadays employed consonants in an almost surrealist manner, she still used them very clearly at the end of every word. He liked it.

"I come from Boston," Hasse said, quickly.

"You can walk along with us for a bit, and I'll show you the way," she said. "I sometimes walk the dogs in that direction."

"They seem very healthy," he said.

Right then, he noticed that he was sweating inside his overcoat, sweating on this cold winter day! There was something frightening about it, something that didn't add up, and he couldn't understand what it was.

"Has Sweden changed a lot?"

"What do you mean?"

"Since you were here last?"

"I've only been here three days this time."

"And when was the last time?"

She walked very quickly, the dogs running loose thirty meters ahead, evidently used to getting along on their own without making a lot of trouble at intersections.

"Late '50s," Hasse said quickly. "It's gotten more expensive, a whole lot more expensive."

"Even if you've got dollars?"

"The hotel rates are crazy. And people dress so oddly, in an almost military manner; everyone in the same kind of down jacket."

"Down jackets, oh, that's the laborers. In the summer they wear clogs. Didn't they do that in the '50s?"

"Absolutely not."

"That's the kind of thing you don't notice when you live here."

She's alive, he thought. However it happened, and it's all very mysterious, she's alive.

"I'm told there's very little initiative nowadays," he said.

"That depends on what you mean," she said. "The whole system strongly encourages individualism and private enterprise to an almost exaggerated degree. Underneath the surface. But for me, who's just a soprano at a music theater, it doesn't matter so much. Well, perhaps it does. But only indirectly. I meet a different kind of people now than I used to."

"Different how?"

"Softer. More low-keyed. Or else very hard. But nobody who makes me feel that life is fun."

"Is that so very different from Massachusetts, where I live?"

"Don't ask me."

"I'm not. I'm asking myself. The last five years, there hasn't been any peace there either. Inflation undermines the forms; the prime rate undermines the houses. I think hedonism in the U.S. is at an end."

"Nobody feels threatened here."

"What's it like here, then?"

"They're quite apathetic. They're neither hopeful nor hopeless. They're convinced that whatever they do, it won't affect their lives very much."

She had a feeling that this whole conversation was basically

128

treacherous. It was theatrical and unneccessary. If he'd wanted to start flirting with her, that would have been understandable, and perhaps also easier to turn down. It had really been a long time.

This half-American walking beside her seemed to want something from her, God knows what, but definitely nothing that would interest her. Their worlds met for a moment. But there was glass in between.

He acted as if he were some kind of detective or spy—it was hard to know, nowadays—but that wasn't the strangest thing about him: that was the way he seemed to bring about landslides in her mood.

Afterward she couldn't remember exactly how their conversation had ended, how they had parted, if he'd patted the dogs or drawn back from them; she only remembered that she sat helpless on the couch, trying to remember herself. (At the same time as she was trying to forget that it was almost time to go to the theater for one of those continual, idiotic, routine supporting parts.) Something yellow, which she did not think came from the gray daylight outside the window, seemed to take possession of the whole room.

The yellow on a kitchen floor in her childhood, in her grandmother's house, sieved through the yellow curtain in the back window. Color before a thunderstorm.

And—she didn't know for which time in her life—something stirred in her. Was it art? Or God? Once everything had been so simple.

When she was a young girl, she never had the feeling of *being a girl*. Nothing, neither people nor the world, had stood between her and art. When she practiced Mozart's Susanna from *Figaro* with the school's woman music director on Sunday afternoons (and still the same yellow light through the curtains) her path went straight into the music. She lived in it with obvious domiciliary rights. She lived, you might say, in paradise in those days.

What lay there between her and that time? What was it that wanted to be born, and what was it that had been born? Now there was just one other bus. If she missed that one, she'd be late for the performance.

129

The unbelievable blindness of the world filled her with sticky nausea. The glue of existence.

Nobody sees me, she thought. It isn't just that no one listens to me; nobody sees me, either. Nobody sees me at all. She watered all the flowers carefully and stayed home from the performance. The telephone kept ringing, and she let it ring.

7

"You wouldn't happen to have the correct time," said the possibly Lebanese woman in the deck chair.

"I don't," I said. "I'm sorry, but I left my watch in the room."

I thought she was a little bizarre with her two black braids, her elegant silk bathing suit, her eternal glass of tea with a slice of lemon, and her delighted, loud laughter as she spoke to the swim instructor.

Now I was looking at her through the tears of my latest coughing spell.

"You shouldn't leave your watch in the room at this hotel," she said.

"No?"

"You never know what kind of people are running in and out of the rooms."

"No, that's true. Have you lived here long?"

"A couple of months. It gets boring after a while."

"Your husband works for UNCTAD, I suppose?"

"No. My husband's dead. I come from Beirut."

"Many people die there."

"Yes, many."

"You're a Christian."

(She wore a small cross on a gold chain around her neck.)

"Yes. Are you?"

"I don't know what to say. I'm Swedish. I come from Sweden, but I've been a tourist guide in Senegal for many years. In Sweden, you don't make that kind of distinction. In Sweden being a Christian is an opinion. With you, of course, it's fate to be a Christian, but among us it's something you believe. And you never know what your beliefs are."

"I've never thought of that," she said.

She seemed less young now, viewed from close up. Her thin legs, her narrow elbows, her long, slender wrists (a gold bracelet hanging from one of them) seemed misleadingly girlish.

"Do you have children?" I asked.

"No, there wasn't time for us to have children. For a long time I had a cat instead, since I wanted to have something I was allowed to touch, but it disappeared."

"Where? Here?"

"No. In Beirut."

"I have a friend," I said, "who considers my relationship to silence too neurotic. I would always interpret silence as disapproval, as something that had to be filled in."

She laughed, a knowing little laugh. She would have been a wonderful woman if she hadn't been so sad.

"I think I've changed now," I said. "I think I've discovered that nothing is better for your body than silence. After having been among many people who talked. By the way, do you know that I was once a poet?"

"How interesting. I remember that I was once very interested, too: in French poetry, of course. I hardly know anything about Arabic poetry. But it's gone now. There is so little world around me now, since my husband died."

"I'm sure that's true," I said. "That the world can disappear. Or else you yourself disappear. When I was a small boy, I often had the feeling that I was disappearing. There was someone the grown-ups talked to, but it wasn't me. The real me had gone away and would never come back."

She was silent, but in an attentive, listening manner. I continued to myself only, however, because this lady was grieved more than I was by the burden of being in the world, and there was no longer any reason to believe that anything I had to say could teach her anything.

From there, my thoughts traveled in many directions. A winter day in the early '60s when, in an early frost that made your breath visible, I stood watching little children being put into carriages by their nurses to ride behind ponies in the Luxembourg Gardens. Small, well, and elegantly wrapped-up bundles, red-cheeked and full of expectation; the nurses jingling small change in their apron pockets; the driver, a big, heavy farmer, perhaps from Britanny; hovering over all this, the beauty of life itself, the beauty of banality, like the beauty of flower pots in a window which, for a moment, had made me completely happy.

It was in the midst of rather an unhappy period: I was going around borrowing money to join my friend in Senegal, and my methods were diverse. I remembered that I had a badly cleaned and threadbare overcoat that day in the Luxembourg Gardens, and a large black slouch hat, and that a small girl got scared of me and ran back to her nurse, who lifted her into her arms.

It was probably only a kilometer from Rue d'Assas, where August Strindberg once lived at the Hotel Orfila, and I wondered what he'd have said about that scene. "All living things serve?"

"Do you think," I said to the Lebanese lady, "that all living things suffer?"

"To be affected by things, to see, somehow always signifies suffering. The Greek philosophers don't distinguish between those two things."

The flower-pot beauty, the banal beauty of life, the beauty of silence. Was there anything else that had really meant anything to me? And was there anything else to concern yourself with?

"Have you ever been to the delta of the Senegal River, up north?" I asked.

"No," she answered. "Unfortunately not. I sit here day after day, like a prisoner, waiting for my brother, who is older than I, to come back and take me with him."

"There are a tremendous number of birds up there. I haven't been myself for a very long time, but I remember it as a superb sight when the pelicans rise, by the thousands, in huge whirls over the river's tributaries and reed beds. They rise like the river of souls rises above the landscape of Purgatory in Doré's illustrations. Through these whirls fly clouds of rose-colored flamingos. You see," I continued, "at certain times the world has a beauty that makes it seem as if it were actually trying to speak."

"Perhaps it's a mistake for you to have stopped there," said the lady, turning toward me, at the same time starting to anoint her right elbow carefully with suntan oil.

132

Her brown eyes glittered with almost childish mischief.

"Perhaps your mistake," she said, "was never getting from beauty to morals."

"And from morals higher up the ladder," I said. "Up to religion? In that case, I'm afraid I share that mistake with all of my generation. Anything but God. People were making a career on the strength of it when I was young, rather the way people would make a career out of a trip to Africa ten years later. I wonder why it was so tremendously important to avoid God in the 1950s? You know, I can't remember."

"You look tired. You speak so eagerly and hectically. Don't you want to rest some, be a little quieter?"

I fell silent. And the poem came to me.

Of course it wasn't mine, but Rilke's, one of Rilke's great *Sonnets to Orpheus*, but it came to me anyway and was mine for a moment. The sea was achingly blue, and a two-masted schooner was going down the coast. In the white breakers outside the overhang, black bodies were swimming, diving time after time from the rock down into the frothing whiteness. How difficult to leave such a world! How difficult it always is, leaving worlds!

> Almost a girl she was, and she stepped forth
> out of this joyous bond of song and lyre
> clearly shining through her springtime veils
> she made herself a bed inside my ear.

"It's really strange," the Lebanese lady said, "but there are things in your personality that don't add up at all. Sometimes I think you're a poet, maybe a great poet, in your own language. Sometimes you're just a tourist guide in Casamance, and sometimes you're some third thing that I can't see at all, can't understand at all. There's something in you that doesn't add up."

"No," I said. "It's quite possible. I don't add up. I've never added up very well, as a matter of fact. I've never had the feeling that I was the one responsible for those connections."

A busboy in a white coat came down to our corner of the swimming pool. He seemed to know her well, since he just said:

"There's a telephone call for you, Madame."

This annoyed me because it prevented me from learning her name. I'd have liked to know it. She rose quickly, gave me an apologetic smile, and disappeared in her short white bathrobe in the direction of the telephone booth by the small lunch veranda at the other end of the pool. The air was vibrating with heat, the schooner had disappeared, not a breeze stirred in the palm trees, but the heavy South Atlantic surf was beating, and the boys over there on the distant rock were still falling into the water like sharp arrows.

Somehow, I thought, she's the only person, no, that's not true, the only woman I've talked to for several months. She's the first person for a long, long time who's talked to me without demanding something from me.

And slept in me. Her sleep was everything.

Why, I asked myself, have I been feeling so strange the last few days? It's as if nothing worried me anymore. Or as if *everything served*.

Half an hour later I beckoned to the boy and put a bill into his hand. He regarded me with calm, benevolent eyes.

"Please tell me the name of that lady."

"What lady?"

I gave him another bill of the same denomination.

"The dark-haired lady who was sitting in the chair next to mine and talked for a while."

"I will ask my colleague, Monsieur."

He disappeared into the little straw-covered hut used by the swimming pool employees, but he returned very quickly.

"Well?"

"Monsieur, my colleague says he's not sure what you're talking about."

"The lady," I said, with a certain bitter sharpness in my tone, "whom you fetched to the telephone a little while ago."

The boy looked as if he were telling the truth; he was embarrassed—evidently embarrassed on my account. He wanted to

134

leave and not continue the discussion. I held him by the elbow for a moment, and I suddenly realized how weak my grip, my handshake, had become in the last few days.

"Monsieur," the boy said, "I assure you there has never been any such lady."

"Thank you," I said.

> . . . Will you create this theme
> before the singing shall consume itself?
> Where sinks she out of me? . . . Almost a girl . . .

This world or another one? A parallel world or the same one? The room was quite empty when I walked in. The door to the balcony was standing open, letting in the sound of the waves. A thunderstorm was gathering over the old slave-dealer island of N'Gor.

Of course he was lying. Either this woman was a visitor from a parallel life, someone who knew me along a different world line, as a science fiction writer would have said (I always read my passengers' sci-fi novels on the Casamance River; I learned a lot that way), or else she was a helper, placed there to see that I got away.

She was a girl, and she had looked in for a moment.

I went out on the balcony to see the storm gather over the horizon . . .

8

Jan had won. This time by dying. He knew it from a friend of his sister's and experienced the relief of the loser.

Hans had a strange habit, one among many strange habits, developed over the years on the Harvard tennis courts. Not altogether compatible with what's expected from a totally rational human being.

When the serve wasn't working, for example, because his partner or else something about the situation made him too self-conscious, he used to solve the problem by dedicating the serve to someone else. He offered the throw to the spirits of the dead, in particular dead tennis players.

Then it might happen that William Tilden, or some other great player, came out of nothingness (that's how he liked to imagine it happening), took over the serve, and swept the ball in a perfect curve, sliced, with a top spin, onto the opponent's side of the court where it landed, unreturnable and mysterious like the darkness from which it had appeared.

That spring, quite a bit later, he drove with his wife and children all the way south by way of Nashville to visit relatives and to discuss a very lucrative offer from Vanderbilt University.

This spring of 1981 felt like a kind of culmination, without his being able to say just why. They were hardly in the Catskills before the nice weather started; it continued day after day until the clouds began to get heavy down in the Mississippi River valley. In the Smoky Mountains the wild cherry blossoms, the honeysuckle, and the oleander looked like an intoxicated *art nouveau* flower painting.

Ver Sacrum, he thought, a holy spring. It goes on somewhere all the time, and the trick is to find your way there.

> "The fairy of a summer long ago
> was holding some white flowers in her hand . . ."

"I wonder how it continues," he said to his wife, who was sitting at the wheel with her round, strong, freshly tanned forearms. She had no idea. She didn't even know which poet it was.

They tried to find a motel in good time each afternoon, so that they had time for a few hours of tennis. They didn't have to be in Tennessee until Saturday. He made the same observation he'd made many times before: it's easier to play tennis in the U.S. the farther south you get. The muscles soften by themselves, there's a dance in the playing that you never got in the dry, cool April air at Harvard.

I've spent the best part of my life in the wrong kind of countries, he thought when the game was 3–2 in his favor in Woodstock, West Virginia. It was an uncommonly pleasant small motel in a little valley by an abandoned railroad, with a backdrop of large blue mountains.

Early spring was far away for him; the whole Swedish trip was nothing but a brief period of black melancholy in a happy, productive life.

There had been something closed-in, something lost, about those days; that's the way you might describe Sweden if you were asked in some faculty club: something closed-in and lost.

Almost without being aware of it, he dedicated his next serve to his old friend Jan Bohman, just as if he were dead, something that was no longer in doubt, and which couldn't be undone.

It turned into quite an excellent sliced serve, which his wife returned from the side of the court. She had a kind of heavy, rhythmic, in the long run very effective way of returning serves.

He couldn't imagine any wife but her. He couldn't imagine any other country to live in but the U.S.; here in this wild, sweet-scented, mild, and poor West Virginia spring he felt that his life had ended up on the right side.

What might have become of me in Europe, in Sweden, with its bad, mismanaged universities, its centrally controlled research, where every professor has some fifty committees over him watching so that he doesn't become undemocratic—what might have become of me in Sweden isn't worth grieving for.

They had played away their destiny themselves. They'll descend to becoming a third-rate industrial nation. Those who aren't mediocrities there, will make themselves into mediocrities. It'll be their only means of survival.

My mediocre shadow walks around there, among the others. The shadow of the one who stayed at home. Or the shadow that remained.

There's just one strange thing about this shadow.

The one who should have become a high-school physics teacher at the gymnasium in Bromma or in Lidingö, the one who should have married Ann-Marie Nöhme and probably divorced her before long.

There's just one thing that irritates me about that shadow.

It's that it feels more real than I do.

Once more he performed the strange rite in the memory of someone who was now dead.

The two girls had come back from the pool: they looked at the game and wanted very much to take over the court.

His serve was returned this time, too.

9

I moved to the Hôtel de la Paix that same night, since I had a strong, intuitive feeling that they were after me. Around three in the morning the fever started, and I dreamed that the large, pale face of the Lebanese lady, a face like a big, just opened flower, a moonflower perhaps, was leaning over me. The dogs barked, the whole block smelled of coal smoke, grilled lamb, and urine; somewhere there was someone playing a small drum to the new moon.

I was becoming seriously ill, something was quite decidedly wrong. It was almost impossible to get up the steep stairs to the next floor of the eccentric hotel, and that was the floor where the urinals were.

I realized I had to get out of the country before I was too weak to do it.

Then the trying wait for the document that I knew I would need in order not to be kept back at the border with all my money.

Down in the street I saw figures in long, white, nightshirt-like costumes waiting for the bus. The naked bulb above the bus stop swung wildly in the predawn wind. Yes, I thought, before my coughing started up again, this planet *is* populated.

Since there was no hope of going back to sleep in the sick dawn, I started to sort through my belongings. There wasn't much I had been able to take along from Ziguinchor, but I'd managed to bring along the big, heavy oilcloth book with my accounts and the small one with poems.

Once upon a time there had been two notebooks of poems, but the first one had been gone for many years.

There was so little I had written the last few years: when I stopped sending back articles it was as if the poems had died, too. It was as if I'd ended up on the wrong world line and no longer could do anything about it. In science-fiction novels it happens that the heroes, when they return from some excursion in time, don't recognize anything: something they did, a butterfly thoughtlessly stepped on, or perhaps a rock they threw that ended up far out in a swamp instead of on dry land, has changed the development of the world in such a way that the one they return to resembles ours quite a bit, but it isn't exactly the same.

It's something like that I'm afraid of.

There were a few damp-spotted, stiff pages left in the note-book, and while I waited for the sunrise, I sat down on the edge of the bed and wrote a poem again, for the first time in six or eight years:

The River Alone Remains

It is possible to imagine God as an
immense Mountain
where everything that falls is still preserved
in the crevices
in the ancient caverns.

All else is water.
Under the whirls of restless birds
(Thus I saw them whirling over my youth's
church steeples
thus the storks still whirl, heavy white spirits,
above the whirls in their manhood's river;
this whirl wants something else.)
the river flows, calm and broad.

In the blood, many a poison
remains, turned to a bitter taste
but time is a Bird Alone
singing across transitory waters.

The life that happened isn't mine,
my own I cannot find.
The river carried all away
The river alone remains.

10

Through Ann-Marie's dream there was a sound as of a coin falling on a marble floor, rotating. With each turn, the note goes up by a fifth. Far in her dream, she imagined how difficult it would be to sing the corresponding scale at a corresponding tempo. The annoying coin was somehow unreachable, and in her dream, a small boy in short pants of green velvet, who no doubt *was* Wolfgang Amadeus Mozart, was running after it, and the boy and the coin were both unreachable.

Since the theater had continued wanting to give her early retirement, she had finally made her decision that spring.

She was now a receptionist in an advertising consulting firm and funneled the visitors into different rooms, answered the telephone with a breathing technique that must have surprised some people, and felt very far away and at the same time strangely relieved.

Now heavy cannon wheels were traveling across marble floors in her dream: evidently someone was pulling old-fashioned artillery, of the Renaissance kind that can be seen at Gripsholm Castle, into a marble palace of the sort where the second act of comic operas usually takes place. She was afraid they'd ruin all the furnishings.

But of course she didn't know how the palace was furnished.

It might be hours, or just minutes, before the alarm went off.

Right now, almost fifty years old, with wrinkles beginning to show at the base of her throat, with the too-lonely woman's faint smell of celery that's been left lying too long in a country cupboard, with a bit of sciatic pain in her right hip, she felt giggly with happiness.

I'm out of it, she thought. Art doesn't make me unhappy anymore: it doesn't concern me anymore.

Most things have been lost in my life, for example everyone I loved. But at the same time, nothing can be lost. Everything has its time and does service there.

I have my health. I'm supporting myself better now than I did at the theater. I'm going to have my piano tuned, because at last I'll be able to play without having a bad conscience.

At last all the melodies will be played.

Without guilt, she thought once more that once she had been very happy. It was that summer with the Bohman boy, who afterward never published another book of poetry. He'd given her such a strong feeling that freedom really existed, although perhaps not for everyone.

There might be hours or seconds left before the alarm went off.

For time is mostly for those who are still hoping.

6   The Song Alone, Retrieved

April 1982 was dry but kindly in Sweden. On the island of Essingen the flower beds already showed some bloom: the bulbs were on their way up, the Highway Department's big street-cleaning machines pulled up the leftover dust of winter, and there was just as much dust in the house. Stickan and Git had decided that now, with spring coming, they'd put the old frame-house in order, the one that had belonged to Git's mother. It was right opposite the Liberal Catholic Church, an appendix to the island.

It had been rented for a couple of years, but the tenants hadn't bothered about it much. Stickan wanted the floors sanded and varnished; Git looked small and fragile on her knees in a corner of the old living room, pulling up the old linoleum, with her blond hair tied in a pony tail.

It was hard work: it was easy to catch your fingers, and when you'd freed sufficiently large chunks of linoleum from the backing, there were always nails and tacks that you'd kneel on.

She was a girl with a lot of go: she and her mother had run her father's bakery on Långholmsgatan for a long time after he died. She was used to hard work, and she was still only twenty-one. Stickan, who was more academic and refined, swore a lot when the pliers didn't want to grab hold of the tacks or when the great chunks of linoleum got too heavy to fold.

The hardest job was carrying them outside, since they were so awkward, and by and by they settled on throwing them into last year's still-brown grass in great pieces that would glide for a bit before they landed.

"Look out for the neighbor's crocus," Git said.

There were so many layers that they told the whole history of the house.

"This is a kind of archeology," Stickan said. "Here's Swedish history back to the '20s."

"Pooh, the top layer isn't archeology," Git said.

"Yes, that too." A kind of thick plastic floor covering, singularly difficult to remove, that Hjalle and Berit had put down one of their last years in the house. It had a kind of moss-green color typical of ugly floor covering in the '60s.

145

Berit was Git's mother and Hjalle her father. The house dated from the '20s, but her parents hadn't lived there that long. They'd moved in in 1950.

"Under the '60s green, which is attempting to turn the hall into some kind of forest, is the '50s linoleum. It's discreet, a light grayish blue. The '50s are always refined, rather discreet."

"Look, here they've put down newspapers."

"Why do they always put so many newspapers between layers?"

"To even it out, maybe? Look, here's *Stockholms-Tidningen* for March 4, 1956. Then we know when they put down the '50s linoleum. It's a lot like the newspapers that spring: riots in the Middle East and stranded cease-fire negotiations between East and West."

"Time always makes me dizzy."

"Here's the green '40s linoleum, and that was made with real cork. They made them nice and thick in those days."

"Look, here's the last layer, look how thin, and what a poisonous yellow . . ."

". . . maybe they thought it'd look like the wood it protected . . ."

". . . here there are more copies of *Stockholms-Tidningen*, and this one tells of atrocities in the Abyssinian war: SWEDISH AMBULANCE BOMBED . . ."

". . . in the Vietnam or Afghanistan of their time . . ."

". . . all gone . . ."

". . . not gone, left with us like all sediments . . ."

". . . now let's see if we can't fold this so we can break off a big chunk, give me a hand will you!"

"I wonder if we'll ever get this thing organized."

She was beautiful, but also terribly dusty by now. The dust stuck to her forehead, where her blond hair was hanging in loose tendrils.

Hjalle had died as early as 1971, and Berit, who was suffering from Parkinson's, had moved into a convalescent home that April.

"I was thinking of Berit," Git said. "How she's doing now."

"But you called her yesterday."

146

"It's just that I'm not sure that she's telling the truth when she says everything's so damn great. She might very well be despondent and pretend everything's hunky-dory at the same time. Her brother was the same way."

"What was the story with him, anyway?"

"Well, he came back from West Africa in the early summer of 1980. The consulate told us he was sick. The whole thing was very quick. I don't know who helped him get home, maybe the same consul, but all of a sudden there he was, at the Sahlgren Hospital in Göteborg, and Mama went down to see him."

"It was lung cancer?"

"Yes, that's what Berit said."

"Did you see him?"

"No, I couldn't get away. But Berit said that it went fast and wasn't all that painful. There were a few write-ups in the newspaper, actually. He was a poet in the '50s."

"Was his mind clear? Could she speak to him?"

"I don't know. Supposedly he was a bit odd. He wouldn't allow any visitors except Berit, things like that. Then he could be a lot of fun, too. He seems to have had a great imagination."

"In what way?"

"In all kinds of ways. Berit used to tell me how he said all the girls in the '50s looked like her, and all of them were called Ingrid. He had notebooks with some poems from Africa."

"What happened to them?"

"Berit has them now."

"Didn't he leave anything else?"

"You know Berit. If he did, she'd never tell anyone. If you've had a bakery in south Stockholm and battled unions and tax people for twenty years, I don't think you're about to tell all and sundry about some foreign inheritance, I can assure you of that."

"No. That's true. If people in this country have learned anything, it's that the state is the enemy and that anarchy is just about the only thing that's respectable."

"But he hadn't written that much, she said. It was mostly fragments. Outlines."

"Not much to publish, perhaps. You say he was a bit odd toward the end."

"Yes, I don't think he'd have appreciated having his poems published posthumously."

"Do you believe the dead can read what we're writing and hear what we're saying?"

"No, I don't."

"But they might be there just the same. As moral necessities."

"We owe them respect, that goes without saying."

He didn't want to argue with her. What he wanted was to make love to her again. That's why he wanted her to be quiet. In the yellow, friendly spring light the shadows from the tree branches played on the yellow wallpaper. He liked it. It reminded him of something in his childhood.

But Git went on anyway:

"You have to have respect for the riddle in other people."

"Why don't you shut the window; it's blown open, and it's stirring up the dust in here."

"Do you want to take a shower?"

"Wasn't the plumber supposed to come by after three?"

"Nonsense, he won't come today either."

"And then we'll make love again?"

"You're crazy. I've got an exam Tuesday."

"You never saw him?"

"Jan? No. Berit saw him, of course, in the hospital. His face was all swollen, and he had those great big melanomas on his face, the kind Europeans can get if they live in Africa too long."

"Was he in a lot of pain?"

"Berit says it was a bit gruesome right at the end, but that it was fast, thank heaven. He seems to have been a bit confused, too."

"How?"

"He seems to have mixed up living and dead people, or talked about them, invited them to visit him in the hospital, indiscriminately. Professors who'd been dead since the '60s, singers long forgotten, rusted long ago . . ."

"Poor thing! It's touching! He thought he was still a celebrity."

"I'm not sure of that."

"But he was quite a well-known poet in the '50s?"

"I think he was better known as a personality than as a poet.

It's a period, an atmosphere. You've got to shut the window now, can't you see that everything's blowing over in the hall?"

"Sure. But why do you sound so angry?"

"Don't you want to take a shower?"

"But how about the plumber?"

"I don't give a damn about the plumber."

In the early afternoon, the wind suddenly died down. The traffic across the Essinge Bridge took on a duller note: the day changed its tack. The couch they were lying on was dusty, too, in spite of all the wind, and they seriously considered going into town, buying a couple of bottles of wine, borrowing a few records, and maybe having a small party right in the middle of the move.

It might be called an unquiet day. On the way to the bus stop Stickan once more returned to the same topic:

"Are they proud of him in the family, or are they ashamed?"

"Neither. They had hopes for him for a while, the way you do with young people, and then everything returned to normal. It'll be the same with us, believe me."

"I don't think so at all. We don't hope for anything, and we've got nothing to lose."

"I think we'll have thunder. We should have taken an umbrella."

"It'll blow over."

"How do we know that there isn't a big glass wall behind the thunderstorm, that there isn't someone back there watching us all the time? How do we know that we aren't part of an on-going experiment in another galaxy?"

"I'd say we don't know."

"Who was that singer?"

"I don't know. Nobody famous."

"How desperately people groped for each other in that generation. If I think of my own parents."

"It was like there was glass between them somehow."

"Perhaps something blinded them, led them away from essential things all the time."

"And what's essential?"

"God. Love. Anything but this."

The bus came; it didn't have very many people. When they got on the bus, they'd already decided they wouldn't have a party. When they looked, there wasn't enough money left.

"You know," he said, "I've got a great idea for a science-fiction story."

"What?" she asked.

"The world perished in the mid-'50s, let's suppose. The big nuclear war came as early as 1956, and we should all be dead, actually. Just rubble and ashes left. But a few people ended up right in the center of the shock waves from the biggest bombs. The energy released was so great that they were thrown into parallel worlds, onto parallel time lines. In those parallel worlds, life has developed more calmly. Humanity has survived a bit longer."

"Umm."

"At a price, naturally. You get back into the ordinary world. You remember nothing of the white light at the center of the explosion, of the shock wave, of the heat. Your removal to the parallel time line has been too fast for you to notice it. But of course you've still got your memories. You remember what the world was like. It's the same way now, just a bit grayer. A bit more mediocre than the way you remembered it.

"Things break faster. The vacuum cleaner doesn't stand up as long as it used to. The politicians on TV suddenly look more mediocre, the factory managers look like gangsters, and they constantly seem to be involved in gangster business, too. The head of state uses openly anti-Semitic arguments in government debates, and the budget looks the way budgets in Latin American states used to, once upon a time."

"I see," Git said. "The man at the gas station doesn't want to wipe your windshield anymore, not because he's rude but just because he doesn't have any idea what he's doing in a gas station."

"All the cabinet ministers seem oddly absent-minded and surround themselves with flatterers with empty faces."

"That's how it would have seemed to Jan if he'd lived, don't you think?"

150

"But that's not how it happened. God didn't want it to."
"You've sure gotten serious!"

It turned into a beautiful evening after all. Later on, they walked all along the Bergsund shore, and he put his arm around her firm, strong waist and talked persistently into her finely shaped ear for a long time, and it was quite impossible to hear what he was saying.

Just her answer:

"No matter what, someone has to come and take a look at the plumbing tomorrow. Otherwise we could have a flood at any time."

A bird moved in the reeds with nasal cries that almost sounded like a girl with an alto voice in her moment of pleasure (perhaps it was), and everything was fine and very good once more, and there was no way out for anyone.

"Isn't it strange," Stickan said, "that there are so few people out on such a beautiful evening?"